FIRE ON
THE HORIZON

FIRE ON
THE HORIZON

SPENCER MOONEY

LIBRARY OF CONGRESS CONTROL NUMBER:		2012915742
ISBN:	HARDCOVER	978-1-4797-0435-4
	SOFTCOVER	978-1-4797-0434-7
	EBOOK	978-1-4797-0436-1

To order additional copies of this book, contact:
Xlibris Corporation
1-888-795-4274
www.Xlibris.com
Orders@Xlibris.com
118532

Chapter I

Awake, it was 6:00 a.m. the alarm was sounding. Morning sure does come quick.

I took a deep breath as I lifted my wife Fallon's arm, which lay across my chest, to enable myself to reach the alarm. After doing so I rolled back to my origin position.

In a blink of an eye she was gone.

Looking where she had been I simply could not believe my eyes. I quickly noticed the light-blue negligee, which she wore to bed the previous night, was still in the same position it had been moments before when her body was there to fill it.

In an instant I was out of bed calling her name as a painstaking search was conducted of the house. Checking each room with infinite care I came to the conclusion she was nowhere to be found.

Was this happening, could someone just disappear into thin air, as she appeared to have done right before my eyes? Or was it a surreal image of my imagination?

Not sure where else to look I stepped through the outside door. That quickly answered the question if our S.U.V. remained parked in the drive. Of course it was.

Screaming her name into the open atmosphere, like a crazed lunatic, I received no answer except for some small bird singing to the morning

All actions ceased when I looked to the breaking dawn. What should have been the first light of day filtering over the hilltop turning the sky gray was instead a horizon of fire mingled in blood. It cast itself across the land bathing all in an illuminate red.

The sight was more than I could bear. I felt faint. Thoughts danced in my head questioning sanity and interrogating my vision's certainty. For the most part I was a skeptic. I did not want to believe my eyes. Some say, "If one can see it then one can believe it." I wanted nothing more than to suppress.

Closing the door on the silence of the house there was an ominous feeling that consumed me. My heart was beating so hard I could feel it in my fingertips. The world around me was too quiet. The beating of my heart was the only sound to be heard.

I broke the silence with one more irrational attempt at screaming Fallon's name . . . No answer.

This house, how it had always felt gratifying, cozy, and so comfortable. Now was surrounded by sensations of being close, hot, and somewhat eerie.

When one is alone, alone such as I, the mind will seem to play terrible tricks. I liked it none at all. Back against the wall I slid down into a crouching position. I struggled with every fiber of by being to imagine what was taking place.

I felt a pain growing inside my stomach. There was a flash of pure emptiness inside my brain. My mouth went completely dry. I tried to wet my parched lips when a fierce pain shot through my brain rendering me motionless for several moments. I thought something must be done, anything to gain control before I completely lost my mind. I had to get up, regroup, and make some sort of effort. Anything!

I made my way back to the kitchen. After retrieving a water glass from the cupboard, it was filled directly from the tap. It rejuvenated me, to some extent, holding the cold water in my mouth and slowly letting a small portion at a time trickle down my throat.

As reality came crashing back into the passive state I was in, I began to shake uncontrollably. Frame by frame I watched the half full glass of water drop to the floor only to break into a countless number of pieces. An ulterior motive presented itself in my racing mind. Hair stood on the back of my neck. As if I had been shot in the heart by an arrow of adrenalin I made a large leap clearing myself from the potentially harmful debris and found myself in a dead run to the bedroom to get dressed.

No more wondering in aimless circles and contemplating senseless situations.

If I wanted to find out what was happening, now was the time to move quickly. Move quickly I did.

My plan of action may have been premature. What I did know was sure. I had to get dressed, get out of this house, and even though there was not a single soul which lived close, conduct a search of the surrounding area.

After putting my pants on, one leg at a time, I slipped my boots on. Not taking the time to tie them, it was ready enough for me. I flashed down the hall at a speed only know to gods.

My attention, at the moment, was on the one thing that granted access to a quicker search than one on foot. It was the keys to my S.U.V., which hung on a hook by the back door.

With my eyes focused on those keys I was high stepping at a fast pace. Lunging through the kitchen, I saw the ceiling, my feet, and then darkness. A long moment passed filled with nothingness.

When my vision became clear I raised my weary head from the ground to take stock of my situation. It took a moment for my eyes to adjust to the light. My situation made no sense to me. I was in a place, to my recollection, I had never been.

Staring above, watching the trees of a forest point their ghostly fingers to a bleak and lonely sky. My head felt as if it was floating in a body of water. At that moment it was as hard to grasp reality as it was to remember how I arrived at such a place. Oh the things one thinks about when in a daze cannot be comprehended, or remembered.

I needed a few moments for my mind to catch up. Catch up to what I was not sure. To clear may be a better way to put it.

So, for a while I just laid there on the damp ground taking in the smell of rotting vegetation and the feeling of being lost.

The only sound was the rustling of leaves in the wind. It was just loud enough to make it hard to hear anything else. Then, off in the distant rolling hills there was the distinct sound of thunder.

In the position I was in, the last thing I needed was to be caught in an unknown place during a storm.

My muscles were stiff making it hard to rise. Rise I did. Even the shift of my eyes brought pain as I searched my surroundings to give myself an idea of which way to start moving.

Before the decision was made, out of the distance like a whisper on the wind, I heard my name. Was that? . . Yes it had to be Fallon calling my name.

For a moment I could only stand in my position. Shifting my head from side to side I tried to figure out which way to go.

Again the call came. I began running in the direction it had come. I called to her many times. Every few steps my direction changed to maneuver around obstacles hindering my frantic search.

Knowing not of where I was made it quite confusing. Everything I saw looked strange, new, the same. For all I knew I was running in circles.

Once more a voice sounded. This time it was more distinct bringing knowledge that it was not the voice of Fallon. This voice was powerful, coming from all directions at once. The voice said something to me I did not understand, yet made my skin crawl across my muscles. It said, "Be afraid; for I am the First, the Last, and you have missed it."

"Who? Missed what?" I answered.

Faintly, as if retreating in the forest it said at last. "The mystery of the Seven Stars, you were warned this time would come."

This statement was far beyond my comprehension. Whoever this was had to be the one that had my Fallon.

Rage began to revolve in my mind. I wanted to take action. What action? I needed to move. Move where? I wanted to scream for help. To whom would I have screamed?

I had to find the strength within myself to overcome my mind and what lay ahead. All for one, so some say. There was no one there but me. What must be done, I could not rely on anyone but myself to do. In the distance I spotted a clearing. I began to make my way in its direction. Every step taken was deft but timid in caution of what was ahead. Feeling plus hearing every dead leaf and twig underneath my feet made it hard to concentrate. Coming closer to the clearing, once again I heard thunder.

My eyes were fixed on the clearing. Were my eyes playing tricks on me or was I seeing movement beyond the tree line? The question started a fast pace. There were rocks in my path that reached waist high. Acting in one motion I took a few large steps, put my palm on one, and threw myself over.

One could imagine my breath-taking surprise when I found abruptly on the other side was a gorge separating me from the clearing. I nearly lunged myself off into it. Fortunately there was a small ledge I landed on. Instantly I broke into a sweat and took a deep breath in relief. The gorge was no more than eighty feet across and ran for as far as my eyes could see from side to side.

The rock wall I was to descend into was not an eminent pitch. If I crouched it was possible for me to slide its depth of twenty feet quite easily. From where I stood it looked as if the other side would not be such an easy task.

My descent was as I predicted, with no trouble. Save a few scrapes on my palms, which were only superficial wounds, of course.

The bottom of the gorge showed no signs of recent use by water or animal. My father, Neol, had taught me many things as I grew into manhood. Two of these I held dear were survival without modern equipment and the art of swordplay.

When reaching the other side I, found my vision had served me correctly in seeing from atop. It was going to take a bit of thinking and ingenuity to master my way to the top of a sheer rock wall.

My eyes searched the rim and I could not help seeing the sky above. So strange, the clouds were patterned like a human's rib cage and were moving at an enormous rate of speed. Now, as strange as that may seem it's not what bothered me. When clouds move quickly one would think wind would be evident. In sound, in the tops of the few trees I could see, maybe the blowing of debris from above, no, just the clouds. I could not waste time on figuring that one out for I had a problem before me that needed my full attention.

I stood a few feet back from the wall studying my options, which were not many. There was not much to see from where I was located. Looking side to side my situation would not improve by scouting through this gorge. There were no ledges to grasp and no boulders close enough to the wall to climb onto in hopes of reaching twenty feet or even giving me a head start.

There was a crack, which ran the entire height of the wall and it was just wide enough to put my foot in if it were on a bit of an angle. Slight protrusions presented themselves for my fingertips, enabling me to worm upward, slowly.

No part of my ascent was easy. After ten minutes, give or take, my feet were only four feet from the ground. My muscles did not ache but my fingers did a bit of complaining.

The higher the ascent, the better I maneuvered. When close to the top I lost foothold and came close to a nasty fall, but recovered nicely. I did a great deal of climbing growing up back in the broken hills and it sure paid off.

Before I realized, there were only a few feet to go. With the hard work and a big reach I pulled myself to the top with great pleasure.

I took no time to rest when reaching the top. My body could have used it, my mind would not allow. I thrust my body into motion, ignoring fatigue, towards a thick line of brush for admittance to the clearing.

Only steps away from my destination again, I heard thunder. Following, somewhat mixed with the thunder was a voice that suggested, "Come and See."

That voice, its power chilled me to the bone rendering me speechless. Morbid curiosity overtook me.

After walking through the last few feet of brush, with a driving force, abruptly it ended and the clearing began. I poised in witness of a city down deep in a valley below the brink where I was standing. The smell of foliage left my nostrils replaced with a smell of carnage mingled in smoke. The city was completely engulfed in flames. Though I was quite some distance from the burning city the screams of its inhibitors filled my ears. People being burned alive make a sound that cannot be emulated nor described.

What could I do? What could anyone have done in a situation such as I was in but turn their back, that's just what I did.

I found myself standing in front of a horseman.

His face was illuminated to a brightness making it impossible to decipher the contours of his face. He was dressed in some sort of white cloak. His horse was also white, not the white known to you and me. It was a white far surpassing any white imaginable. In his hand he held a golden bow.

In the instant of realizing his presence I felt a slight tickle on my upper lip. My nose was bleeding profusely. My only reaction was to stare at this power being.

Pulling an arrow from the quiver, strapped to his back, he notched it deftly to the bow's string. He pulled it almost effortlessly, took aim, and released.

Some say in times like that one's life passes quickly in their mind, not I. There was only a single picture I could recall. As you may have guessed, the picture was of my beloved wife. How was I to find her, help her, if I were to be slain? No time!

The arrow pierced my chest with monstrous force. In an instant I was flat on my back gasping for air. I pulled helplessly on the golden arrow in my chest. No good, stuck in bone, too late.

Shadows crept towards me as I could only let them come. Darkness consumed my sight and I was left where the sun dare not go. Twisted thoughts of what was to be filled my dithering mind. By body began to shake violently as the taste of death touched the tip of my tongue and worked its way throughout my inner being.

Trying not to bother myself with questions concerning why me, or how can this be happening for I would have none of it. I was a fighter. Life inevitably has an end but I wasn't finished. I would not accept death that day.

I spat the death from my mouth as if it were a mouthful of soured liquid.

A flash of colors swam into my vision. Fresh air filled my lungs. I fluttered my eyes and it seemed to only hurt my head, it did nothing for my vision.

I was cold, cold and numb. The darkness had returned and was pitch as night. Reaching out my hand I could feel only emptiness. Ignorance is bliss.

Was I dead? Not dead, the numbness was leaving me and was replaced with pain. If pain could be felt then it was an indication of life, for life is pain.

11

Bright spurts of light entered my field of vision as I fought myself back to consciousness.

My skull was throbbing with every pulse of my heart. I had to sit up.

Rising to a sitting position, I gently ran a hand over my chest. No arrow? Not even painful. Something was not right about my skull. Carefully inspecting my head with light touches I came to the spot in question. When touched it shot what felt like a bolt of electricity down my spine through my legs and blew out my toes.

I had something there embedded in my skull. It felt like . . . it was a piece of glass.

Realization came flooding back. Dropping the glass of water completely escaped my memory when I started for the door. I was in my kitchen floor. How long I had been unconscious from the fall I did not know. The dream of the burning city and the horseman haunted my thoughts.

With every moment passed my mind regained clarity. Consciously bound to thoughts of finding out what happened to Fallon made every move quicken, yet, my fall in the kitchen made me cautious.

First things first, as they say, the glass in my skull had to be removed. Then it needed a good cleaning and I was certain the agitation would start the bleeding again. Gauze and the right amount of pressure should be adequate. Under the sink in the bathroom was the proper aid for the job.

After making my way to the bathroom, stepping in, and making a move for the cabinet I gave myself a sharp glance in the mirror before me, I froze. The image projecting back filtered through my eyes but did not register in my brain as my own. The eyes looking at me lacked substance. They were opaque and hallow, seeming to be an open window to a soul of darkness. The skin on my face was pale and thin.

"Rizon" I said out loud "boy, you look like left over death."

Tearing myself away from the pitiful image I retrieved the proper treatment supplies and began work on my head.

Chapter II

Nearing the finishing touches on doctoring my wounds my gaze fell up on a space on the wall where, for as long as Fallon and I had built the home, a symbol had hung. Not just any symbol but a probable clue to the disappearance. It was a crucifix. All that remained was dust and the stain of life that had surrounded it.

I was a skeptic and was more of a neutral party in subjects concerning religious conviction. Fallon was a believer but as for me I was sure religion was merely bedtime stories made to keep a certain balance. Fables created mostly to keep children out of mischief. Preposterous it had anything to do with my wife's disappearance. As quickly as the thought had appeared in my wavering mind I tried to suppress it.

It was the only explanation that actually made any sense. The clarity of the situation brought me to my knees. Not to do what one might think I should have done, at the time, for I knew it was far too late for that.

Thinking back to the fall in the kitchen brought back a painful realization. My vivid dream had harsh meaning. It was far beyond my comprehension at that time, but now . . .

There was no time to rake myself over the coals too much for at that instant effluvium entered my nostrils.

Looking at me in the mirror wide eyed in disbelief I inhaled deeply. Yes without doubt, smoke. It was wood smoke amongst other burning materials, so strong I could taste its acridness.

Turning to exit the bathroom I could see an immense cloud of smoke billowing down the hallway. There was so much smoke it was impossible to tell which way it was traveling from. It looked as if the fire could be at either end of the house.

I made my way down the hall toward the kitchen in a half crouched position. Only a few steps were made before an uneasy feeling affected my pursuit of escape. I must have hit my head harder than I thought for my equilibrium was skewed.

I went down to one knee as my vision blurred. From the smoke or my condition I was not sure, nor cared. All I knew was I must get out.

Glancing into each room as I pasted, I concluded the fire had to be in the room of living or the kitchen.

Black spots appeared before my watering eyes as my throbbing head swam. My mouth was dry and I was rapidly suffocating.

Entering the passageway to the kitchen I could also see into the living room. The big question was answered but it did not help my situation. The fire was coming from both. The house's exterior was bleeding fire through the ceiling. Fallen portions of the ceiling had caught drapes, walls and other materials into flames causing a nearly impassible fire gauntlet.

Ambiguously smoke hung overhead in a thick cloud. Flames crackled and licked out at me with malicious intent.

Bobbing and weaving to avoid the flames lavish tongue I made my way through the kitchen, over the broken glass and dried blood to my keys.

At the moment I retrieved my keys from the hook on the wall my exit was cut off from the outside. The wood porch outside the back door came crashing down with force and flames. For the moment I felt loss of hope as if those events were no accident. Maybe it was a quick severe punishment for lack of dogma. Cynical, at times, I may be but my proof surrounded me.

Making my way through the living room was not as hard as the kitchen. The heat and smoke still penetrated to my inner being but all thoughts ceased after bursting out the front door.

It was hailing as far as my eyes could see in all directions. Not a hail, to my knowledge, ever documented in times past. The pea size hail was on fire. Each individual peace projected a blue flame setting fire to the land and wasting my dreams.

Somewhat protected, for that moment, by the imminently pitched roof of the porch, I froze. A piece ricocheted off the railing and bounced near my foot. Though I knew full and well its ramification if touched, it made no matter. I reached, as quickly as it had come it was gone rapidly burning out leaving a charred spot before me.

How long would this storm of hail fire last? I could not wait. My house was burning down around me and I had to move. The only option, I was aware of having, was to make a run for my vehicle. I removed the aluminum trash can lid residing beside me for a shield readying myself for a last chance of escape or directly into my demise.

Holding the lid above my head I made for my S.U.V. twenty-five steps, or should I say leaps, landed me directly beside my destination. With a flash of open and close I was inside. Unmolested I was, save a small burn on my elbow. As crude as my shield was, I remain quite surprised I sustained only the small burn.

When the blood flows, through a bodies veins as mine had, it will set one's mind into a terrible twisting motion causing bone chilling, hair rising, excitement beyond belief.

Life is full of challenges. If those events wanted me dead they were going to have to make a better play than that to take my hard earned life. It was not ever in my nature to fathom such a thought as to give up.

Motionless, even more I was helpless. Helplessly watching my home and the life I had known become nothing more than a charred ruin while sitting in my vehicle. The hail fire had stopped falling from the sky. Then the sky turned to a state of normality as havoc remained. Most of the trees and grass on that unforgiving day was but ash withering away, taking my dreams and life with it in a slow wind.

The claw of depression held me tight in its grip. Every breath it grew tighter, with every thought tighter still. Squeezing the steering wheel until my knuckles were on the verge of detonation, I fell.

I fell deep within myself in search of an answer. An answer to a question I was not sure even existed. At that point my mind had lost all reason.

For a moment, a very long moment, I sat in a daze. Rain had come to follow the hail fire and as the rain lifted so did my daze.

My clothing was filthy. Soot lay heavy on my skin. Rubbing my face with my palms I felt a sting of pain. Bringing my hands away from my face I saw my palms were moist. Looking into the rearview mirror I could see the heat from the house fire had blasted my face to blister. I was a complete mess.

Wild the wind and strange was the path that lay before me, yet not as strange as the thoughts conjured in my mind. Feeding off the strange illusions in my mind I became enveloped in a wave of despair as I drove away from my home.

Denial is for the indecisive and not being able to make a decision is for the feeble. I was neither. Fallon had disappeared, that was a fact. The fire burned my home and nearly everything in sight, also fact. Situations were bad and going to only become worse was a sick realization but also fact. So I set my sights on the city.

The nearest city was miles away over twisted broken hills and it was there I had to go.

For every beginning there must be an end. Now who is to say there will ever be an "End to this world"? For the planet, it will always exist. The events that had been taking place were shaping up to be the end to the life as it was to be known.

My objective was to go to the city and find my brother. Unless some miraculous change had come over my brother I was certain he had not been taken. We had not spoken in a while for no other reason than being wrapped up in different lives. I knew if I could find him the two of us together would figure out some way to survive which was to come.

Static was all I had received on the radio as I drove. My cell phone! I had not thought of my cell phone. Digging it out from under a few items in the passenger seat I saw no signal. Dead zone, the term rang true. No matter, once I reached the city questions would receive answers.

Trouble had settled around me like a blanket. The feeling inside told me it was not going away for a very long time.

Crossing bridges in desperation, seeking in a world of, "What if?" I drove. When stating the term crossing bridges it's not literal, though some may have literally been crossed, I mean bridges in my mind. I was enveloped in future events taking place in my mind. They were situations that may or may not even happen. Every angle, countless possibilities I conjured and turned over then over again in my mind. Thoughts consumed me to the point I scarcely remember miles I had driven.

I pulled my way back to reality just before the impact. One should not ever think that life cannot get worse than their present, for it can find a way to do so.

Crossing those imaginary bridges I had missed a jog in the road and came head on with a power line poll. Thinking back I had been driving at about 60 miles per hour before my actions lost themselves in the darkest corners of my mind. Just before the hit my eyes passed the odometer, noticed 75 miles per hour, the poll, and then the impact.

Sure enough my seatbelt was not fastened and my face hit the windshield sending blood in all directions. The vehicle flipped end over end, only once, leaving me down side up. I had gripped the steering wheel so tight that when my body was thrust into it the column broke.

Situating myself in a better position I took stock of my condition. My fingers and toes worked, all other joints seemed to be in order. My nose was broken. For some strange reason, one I may not ever know fully, I laughed. First time with a broken nose may have brought a refreshing feeling to experience its sensation. Or quite possibly the head trauma I had received that day had drove me daft.

After quickly resetting my nose I found the impact jammed the doors to a point of malfunction. My choices were few, the back or front glass. I chose the latter. Three or four swift kicks granted me access out of my twisted metal coffin.

So, there I was in a barren wasteland with my vehicle totaled and only my beating heart to keep me company.

Chapter III

A slow desolate trudge took me towards the city. The city was nearly 100 miles away. What condition the city was in I could only guess. Surely had to be better than where I presently was.

Fire scorched land beneath my feet, eerie sky above. Ash stirred with the slightest breeze making it hard to breathe. Though tempered in hard ways, the unforgiving predicament upon me was going to be a great test of my ability to survive. Over and over in a low murmur I told myself "I shall see the city." It was a good thought, one that kept me moving.

I was close to 40 miles away from any known body of water and homes were just as scarce. To survive one can go days without food. In this dry heat one cannot last long without water.

My pace was quick for the first few miles. Noticing my body perspiring profusely I slowed. No easier way to dehydrate one's self than that. Setting small goals and accomplishing them will lead one in a direction of accomplishing the big goals.

For a moment in the distance I could see hills and a sun that was doing its best to make it to the setting position. With optimism and my pace I was confident I could make it to those hills before nightfall. With help beyond the forces of my control I would find a catch or two that held water.

It may have made more sense to some to stay on the roadway on my journey to the city, not me. For the road's direction led further away from the city before it made its way back to avoid those hills. I had seen not a soul traveling that whole time, which was not unusual.

Wonders danced in my aching head while mysteries of an unsolvable nature questioned my waiting mind. The shadow of unforgettable memories hung over me as if it were a starved beast prolonging my end with a snarling smile. Briefly, oh so briefly, did I wish the accident I had just endured had taken me as swiftly as my love had been taken from me. The thought did not resonate long for I was a fighter.

The brutality of the day lay heavy on my muscles, cruel loss hard on my mind. The silhouette of accomplishment was near but being a man of no illusions I knew they were still miles away when day turned to night.

The landmarks had lost themselves with the light. My only way of navigation was to pick a star in the direction of the hills and keeping my eye fixed on it while moving forward.

Stopping a few times to enjoy the coolness of night and catch my breath helped. Thirst lay heavy on my tongue. I had heard somewhere when one is without water it helps to put a pebble in the mouth to keep saliva flowing. Fumbling on the ground one was found and help it did.

I needed sleep as much as I needed water. To fall asleep in the open could have meant death for I could not have been sure the hail fire would not return. Finding my star I awkwardly pressed on.

An uncalculated amount of time brought me to the bass of those twisted hills. So, into the wooded hills I went to seek what comfort could be found.

By the feel of the trees, smell of the surroundings, and what little could be seen not all had been laid to waste by the wrath of hail fire. That alone gave a minute fiber of hope.

Scouting the hillside for shelter was a great task indeed. After stumbling over fallen snags and nearly poking an eye out (twice) with low hung branches, I came to a rock face.

Finding an overhang protruding not more than three feet I came to the quick conclusion it would be sufficient. Brushing small debris from my makeshift place of rest took no time at all and even less time to fall out of consciousness.

Opening my eyes to a day well on its way and myself well enough alone, I stretched. Feeling what the day before had done to me I shuddered to think of what was to come. I tried not to worry much about how my body felt, simply for the reason that if I did not find water soon, I would soon enough be dead. Not willing to accept dying of thirst as my fate I moved on.

Each step brought new obstacles and over every hill was another. Water was a dream.

Why I had decided to move to such a remote location was a question I had asked myself many times. Before those moments, it was in my mind that peace and serenity came with solitude. For those moments it only brought misery and grief. With that knowledge I took another step.

Visually searching my surroundings, something in the distance caught my eye. When one is in an environment of undefined objects and the hard line of a defined shape presents itself, it holds one's attention. Crouching slightly to clear my line of sight I was elated to find the sight was true. There was a house approximately one half mile away.

Excitement overcame my feeble willingness to function properly and I fell hard.

Tenacious effort brought me to my feet and the same effort later brought me to the house.

It was not in me to have made a detailed description of the house. My only recollection was it looked quite simple and well used. My concern was not the house, it was what was inside. It did look desolate and my hope for human contact, slim. Alone and desperate my way was made to the door.

Knocking repeatedly no answer was given. I tried with all that was in me to call out but my throat was too dry to comply with a demand of making words formulate. It was hopeless.

Though my voice would not comply with my need for speaking I had other senses top shape. My ears gave evidence of a lonely manner as my eyes looked through the window with no movement to hold my gaze. My nose could smell no further than my retched self. My time for rational action was up. My strength was failing fast. With my remaining gumption and the only sense left, I took a large step, thrust my shoulder forward, and burst through the door.

I had felt what I was feeling before. The silence of the house brought back painful memories of my own home. The life force the home once possessed was lost as well.

Wonders of the world danced in my mind as I made my way to the kitchen. The faucet was running at a moderate rate, after seeing it there was no thinking beyond my need, I drank deeply.

Turning around something on the floor caught my interest. There was a white night gown and blue apron in a pile. Picking the pile up to inspect further I found slippers underneath. Out to the left side of the pile a wedding ring lay lonely.

The realization of the prophecy sank deep within my inner core and rang true. They left this world just as they were brought in, body and soul.

I lost myself in a moment of thought when the image of my parents and their home cut my mind. I had full understanding they were gone as well.

Those I loved . . . gone; all I owned . . . no more—save my brother. If I knew Lexter, as I was sure I did, he was not taken and I hoped he remained in the city. I needed to prepare. Those people whom resided in that house had moved on. I was positive their earthly possessions did not matter to them. It was vital to my survival.

I had all I needed packed by the door. I had used their facility to wash up and the man of the house was fortunately close to my build so I had fresh clothing. I was running on a full stomach and partially rested when I heard the noise of an approaching vehicle. The smile on my face dissipated as quickly as it came when the thought of human interaction entered my mind.

The young male making his way to the house was not going to enjoy the fact I was there, and even more taking supplies.

I have always been a straight-forward kind of man. The fact I was an intruder taking supplies, did nothing to change the fact. I stood in the living room in hopes he would understand and let him come.

When he came through the door he meant business. I did not even have enough time to utter a word before he clenched his fist and took a swing.

His passion was true, his mark was not, for I simply leaned back slightly and he missed greatly. The man must not have done much fighting in his day or if so he was not on the best end of the deal. His miss through him off balance and I made my move.

Locking his neck in my arm, I took him to the floor. My intention was not to hurt, only to momentarily sedate and try to reason with him. He was strong I'll give him that.

"My name is Rizon. I was near death and needed water. I . . ."

Before I could finish he cut me off with a chocking attempt at saying, "I don't care who you are, I'm going to kill you."

"Not today mister and not ever by the hand of a fool such as yourself." With that being said I tighten my hold.

Only seconds had passed when his muscles went limp. As they did my hold was released. I did not want to leave him there, even worse I did not want to be there when his consciousness returned. I took the supplies, walked out the door, and found my way to his car.

Preservation of one's self is something that motivates humans to do unimaginable things. I am not proud of what I did that day to survive. As I drove the thought occurred to me astutely, it was going to get much worse.

Life can throw one into a monstrous mess time and time again. The best a body can do is take what is left, then take another step. When people begin to tell themselves; "Life can get no worse," it will prove them wrong. If it were as bad as it could be the mind would not function well enough to recognize the difference.

Many miles I drove. Not one moment passed that I did not notice. I had some sort of heightened awareness. When coming within a few miles of the city, I noticed many vehicles exiting the city, but not one going the same direction as I. It mattered not; I was on a mission, a mission to find my brother.

Chapter IV

It seemed no time passed when the city came into view. I had not used any supplies from the house back in the woods, except for a few drinks of water, which I enjoyed every time it touched my lips.

Noticing all cars exiting the city and only myself entering made me wonder if I had made the correct choice. No matter, I needed to find my brother. With our heads together we were sure to find a solution.

Nearly a bird's eye view gave me the answer to the city's condition. Fire induced havoc. Fear produced a pain creeping from the pit of my stomach and presented a foul taste in my mouth.

Fuel was short in my stolen vehicle. So, first exit that with promise, I took it.

People were running crazy. Twisted burning piles of metal, sure to be a vehicle in resent time, were scattered throughout the streets. It was all I could do to make it to the filling station; only to find it abandoned, looted, and in poor shape.

Trying several pumps and receiving no fuel, I was close to admitting failure when he came.

The man looked ordinary, for the most part, but what caught my eye was that he was carrying a five-gallon gas can. Gas was quite expensive to begin with. This was going to be interesting and hard on my wallet.

Turning to square myself with the oncoming man I could tell this man was a person I wanted nothing to do with and the look in his eyes revealed a snake-like demeanor then a price left his tongue.

"100 dollars," the man said, without a flinch or resistance.

"For five gallons of gas, are you insane?" I said, as the negotiation began.

"Not likely to find it anywhere in the city for less, if you find any at all," the man said quite confident.

"All I have is 30 dollars to spend on fuel," lying as best I could.

"Then you had better get used to walking." As he turned to walk away I could tell this man was not going to budge far from his original stated price.

So I made final offer, "80 bucks man, give a guy a break."

The man turned his head so quickly I thought he was going to break his neck. When I saw the look in his eyes blood began to run cold and race through my veins.

In one swift motion he dropped the gas can, reached in his waistband and pulled a knife.

It was evident the man had no intentions to make a deal. All he was after was money and when the statement was made that's all he needed to hear.

This is what it had come to. In a city I did not want to be in, facing a deranged lunatic to fuel a stolen car.

The man was coming so quickly thinking was not an option. My natural reaction took effect. Natural reaction mingled with self-preservation will cause one to do unnatural things.

A few short steps put the man within reaching distance. He did much more than reaches. Thrusting his eleven-inch blade with malicious intent gave me the opportunity I needed.

He went for my midsection with all his concentration and might. My left hand guided the blade and my right index finger sunk deep into his eye socket. It is near impossible to fight without the sense of sight.

With a squeal he was finished, but I was not. His weapon of choice hit the ground by force of gravity making a familiar sound. By doubling over covering his bloody eye, the pain was made evident. In thoughts of helping the man forget about the eye by infliction pain on other areas I began to work him over.

First was his knee. Hyperextension seemed more than suitable. When I came down on it with my boot it sounded like a shotgun going off. He screamed so loud I thought the entire city, in all its chaos, stopped for a moment.

Next I kicked him directly in his fool mouth in hopes of toning him down a notch. Soon after the kick he was short a few teeth, unless he had picked them up later from where he spat them out.

It was time for me to finish him and stifle my aggression. I grabbed a handful of his hair; tilted his head back, and spoke words he was going to remember.

"You brought this upon yourself and deserve it all," with that being said I took the last of the fire out of the man, and his good eye.

I took a few deep breaths to calm myself. A momentary daze flooded my mind with thoughts of what should have been and what needed to be done.

Fuel, I needed the fuel and to find my brother. With those objectives I made my way for the gas can. Some had spilled on the ground and looked peculiar. I touched my finger to the liquid then brought it within range to smell and that told me exactly what I did not want to know. Water!

Not only did the man, who was now blind and choking on his own blood, try to kill me he fooled me as well. My temper was set to fire burning deep within my being, quickly turning itself to rage. I lost it.

Standing from my hunches I ran as fast as my legs would take me directly towards the man. He was on all fours still spitting blood and particles of teeth. I kicked him in his gut with all the strength I could muster. I began to hit him repeatedly and actions in those next few moments were unbeknownst to me. When I regained my vision I was still beating him relentlessly. Suddenly I stopped. The realization of how close I had come to sending this man to his death still shortens my breath.

At that moment words from my upbringing rang my ears. "After the coming all which was once good on this earth will be taken as well."

It was true, all that was pure had been taken, even the thing we all take for granted most of the time, our conscience.

It was far beyond my control to deal mentally with happenings within those city's walls. That is where suppression plays its role.

Suppression is a vital key to survival. When a situation is presented far too great for the mind to accept one will suppress.

It was in my best interest to leave the city quickly. So, with haste I continued my mission.

Pulling out, back on the street, in route to my brother's house the fuel light in the car came on. It bothered me slightly for I knew I had enough fuel to make it to his house but no further than that. Then I would be stranded.

A few blocks down the road an ominous feeling began to creep its way into my mind. It was taking over my will to think clearly. Thoughts of my life before that seemed simple, yet, more confused. I wanted it back but knew it would not be.

I wanted no more than to be what I was. A transformation was taking place. I had to become something I did not ever want to be. Though, in life how many times does anyone ever become what he or she wants to be?

The shadows were growing long and I knew when the day was exhausted I would be too.

Burning buildings, wrecked cars, and dead bodies flashed horror of what the city had become. As if all inhibitors were at war with themselves.

Lootings, shootings and murder set the standards for the strong and brought extinction to the weak.

Many times over I turned my thoughts. I did not feel sorry for what I had done to myself, ashamed . . . maybe. Yet when all the chips were in I could look back on something that made me overly elated, at least Fallon had taken her own path.

> Lost love of mine—can you take the time
> To learn what has become—to forgive of which I've done?
> All has changed—nothing seems the same
> Beyond the memories of youth.
> When we were both together the flame of love burned true.
> Lost thoughts of heaven and hell—I somehow let pass by,
> We stood tall—while others failed the never ending lies,
> No matter what happens to the sky or sea,
> You gave me reason—my only reason to be,

Dreams of my lost love—my lost love and me,
Her eternal life—I've fallen short of what was meant to be.

Those words crashed my conscience with an emotional shattering effect. What was a guy to do but keep on moving on with the little sanity left?

My brother's home was near when night had taken over. The scent of evil was stinging my nostrils and made my eyes water a bit. Well, I guess it could have been the evil or those words repeatedly haunting my mind.

An enormous sigh of relief exited my being when my brother Lex's house entered my field of vision. It was still standing unmolested by the wrath of hail fire.

I became concerned when I noticed most every house in my view had an indication of life; my brother's did not.

After proceeding to the door a disturbing attribute stopped me dead in my tracks. The door was ajar.

The door swung on its hinges with a light kick from my boot and opened to a lonely deserted house. All was still; the aroma brought mental flashes of Lex. Entering gave an undesired feeling, one a person should not feel when entering the home of one's blood.

Though I well knew my next action was useless before the act was committed, it was done anyway. I called his name in a monotone voice with only a shred of hope an answer would be given. There was none.

Rustling noises grasp my attention. The sound was coming from the back room. I was in no mood for games and with stealth I moved closer to its origin.

It was dark in his house but I knew the layout as well as the depths of my mind. The carpet was soft under my feet making sound minimal.

With each step the rustling grew louder as did my beating heart. Oh how I was sure the sound of my beating heart would alert the intruder.

Behind a partially closed door the sound slowed, my pace did not. I burst through the door with no opposition ready for anything except for what I found.

There she was bright and beautiful as sure as a morning star. I did not know who she was but my rage turned quickly into empathy.

Her reaction and the sound escaping from her lungs quickly told me she was as surprised to see me, as I was her.

I'm sure the look on my face is what calmed her. As her gaze held an eyebrow raised and smile slightly broke from her pouting lips.

The look was enough to melt even the hardest of hearts, warm the coldest of cold. Maybe it just felt good to see someone pure after witnessing so much chaos.

"Who are you and what are you doing here?" I asked in as calm of a voice as I could.

"I am Malloy. We have not met yet, I already know much about you. Lex and I have been seeing each other for several months."

24

"Where is he?" the question spouted out of my mouth as I accepted her to be telling the truth.

A look of despair came over her, a look that nearly turned me inside out as she spoke. "I thought I was ready." A teardrop fell from her picture perfect eye.

"Ready for what?"

She sat abruptly on the bed; head hung low and began to confess. "To be taken! Your brother left the city because he thought, we both thought, I was living the way I should. But I guess now it is quite evident, I was wrong."

"Well I am sure you are not the only one who in this predicament." No more did the words roll off my tongue, as I knew it was the wrong statement to make.

She stood erect. "Is that supposed to make feel better?"

"Look doll, I have not the energy to fight. I was only trying to relate. Forgive me for being crude." My brother not being in his home nearly drained me of all my strength so I made my next statement. "My suggestion is to get some sleep and we will make reservations to figure all out in the morning, okay?"

With a look that drove deep into my core she told me "I don't want to sleep alone."

"Well you won't have to. You sleep in the bed and I'll take the floor."

With that said she seemed to be sufficed and we made ready our sleeping places. I made one more pass through the house making sure all windows and doors were secure. Without hesitation sleep was underway as dreams of death and unlived life arrived.

Dark waves lapped over my throbbing skull. The smell of water and carnage filled my soul. Towering above me was a warrior atop a fiery red horse shouting orders. The thought of my death consumed my being as I rose from a place that should have been my grave.

The sound of breaking glass shook me to my core. Setting erect in my sleeping place I took stock of my situation. Softly spoken words from Malloy entered my ears. "They have come for us."

Quickly my way led to the front of the house where I was sure the sound originated. My breath came in short spurts. The intruder must not hear me.

Light steps took me closer to the sound of man and the smell of evil smothered in alcohol.

My eyes were adjusted to the darkness giving me an astute sense of awareness when I found the intruder.

This being, this sorry excuse for a human was doing his best to find footing on the broken glass filled kitchen floor. It took me only a minute moment in time to decide what to do with such filth. It was to break him.

His back was facing, taking three steps I had him in my grasp. Grabbing him, in his full surprise, by the scruff of his neck I spun him half circle and threw him with all my might into the opposing wall.

Something was amiss. I had tangled with many men before. The weight was not right.

Quickly, I turned on the light exposing the travesty of which I was to endure. A boy!

Not much more than the age of fifteen years, this boy. This was just what I needed, an intoxicated adolescent stumbling around in my brother's kitchen in need of a savior.

It was all I could do to keep myself from severely hurting this boy. So, I did what most people should do in a situation such as this. I took two steps and with most of my strength, put my boot directly in his southbound end.

The sound escaping from his lungs answered the question if the point was made. His muscles gave and without motion he dropped to the floor with a light thud.

The boy was unconscious; I think his head hit the wall when I kicked him. Being an untrusting man, I tied the boy with the nearest cord found and made my way to Malloy.

She was peaking out of the doorway inspecting the situation far before I made my way back. The words she spoke stopped me dead in motion.

"Rizon he is my little brother".

I sat directly on the floor in the hallway to ask the first question that came to mind. "Does your little brother have a problem with doors?"

The words that came out of her mouth I could not tell, for I was too involved with my inner struggle. Not only was I to take care of myself in this time of tragedy and despair, now there were two others.

Before the boy woke from his unconscious state he was untied and put on the couch. Malloy sat close by his side watching, dabbing his forehead periodically with a wet cloth. When he finally came around the alcohol had loosened its hold and he was tolerable. My attention to his situation was paid in short, for I had more to worry about.

Gathering supplies into my brother's spare Jeep, I stopped for only a moment to answer a question from Malloy. "Are you going to leave us here?"

"My intentions are simple, to leave this city. It is your choice to stay or go."

"We're coming but where will we go?"

"I am thinking Lex made his way for our parent's house, it is far from this city and it should be safe."

"Can I do anything to help?" She said, with a beauty that made it hard for me to breathe.

"As a matter of fact there is. Take five unbreakable containers, fill them with water, sack them, and then stow them in the Jeep."

"Done deal."

As she returned to the kitchen to start her task, she screamed my name with brutal force.

Making my way as fast as possible I saw what caused her disturbance. Her brother, glass of spilt water by his side, was on the floor convulsing.

The spilt water held attention. Quickly I grabbed a clear water glass, turned to the tap, which was still running and poured it full to inspect further. What was found dislocated my thoughts thoroughly.

Small worms completely consumed the water's surface area. The only thing I have ever seen that looked close to this relevance was the larva of mosquitoes.

Small worms twitching, squirming, acting as if being charge with electrodes filled my sight. Dropping the glass in the sink hearing it break with gravitational force, I slide my arm under her brother Eanin, and started work on him.

Placing him on his stomach I administered the Heimlich maneuver. Two strokes merited his loss of fluids. It was all I knew to do, all I could do. So, from then all that was left was the waiting.

Not long after his breathing became regular and his eyes fluttered a bit. It was sign enough for me to know, if his will were strong enough, he would pull out of it.

We needed sorely to be rid of that twisted city and all it despondencies. The last items to make ready were loaded. Soon after, we three were making our way.

My mind was more than uneasy. I had a knot in my gut and I had a feeling it was not going away for quite some time.

Chapter V

Thoughts weaved through the catacombs of my wavering mind as Malloy spoke of the way life should have been. It's really a shame we all don't make more preparations for future events before they fall upon us, making us wish we had done something different.

I pushed those thoughts deep into suppression as the downtown area came into view. Sickness grew within my being to see the havoc bestowed by the cities own residents.

Doing my best to make hast in finding the best way out of the present hell we were in a situation presented itself of grand proportion. Violently the ground began to shake. Buildings in the downtown area crumbled without hesitation as I was nearly shaken off the road.

"Earthquake? This city doesn't have earthquakes!" Soon after Malloy stated the obvious the quake subsided. Stepping out of the Jeep to survey the damage with a 360-degree view many other travelers followed suit. All that could be seen in the surrounding area had changed by the quakes devastation. Every bit of breath escaped my lungs when I noticed the enormous crevasse that divided the entire downtown area.

We were all in some sort of hypnotic trance by the sight and moments passed unnoticed. Aberration held our gaze; silence held our tongues as the great crevasse began to convulse and spew black smoke darkening the sun. Screams came like a terror in the night. The smell of death stung my nostrils as Malloy and I quickly made our way back to the Jeep, Eanin did not follow.

Just before the sun was completely blackened by the escaping smoke Malloy screamed "Dear God, what is that?" Looking at the base of the pit I saw what caught her attention and caused her dismay. Billowing out of the pit spewed a swarm of insects. They were too far away to tell what type, the sound they made was not known of this world.

Only moments passed before the swarm enveloped the crowd gathered on the side of the street. They swatted, screamed, and ran but the insects tore into their flesh like hungry animals without question or conscience. After screaming her brother's name in exasperation Malloy started out of the Jeep, "Look." I said, as I pointed my finger in a definite direction.

Barely visible through the chaos and swarm came Eanin walking towards the vehicle as calm as a summer's day. The closer he came; more the questions swam in my wandering mind. He climbed in with quickness. Turning in her place Malloy asked the questions that were the only questions to ask, "Aren't you hurt? How you did that without getting hurt?"

As he scratched his wrist looking indifferent he answered in a monotone voice, "I . . . I have no idea. The locust came, I started to run but they only swarmed around me. Not once did one land on me. The other people, did you see what they did to them?"

Malloy answered his question with a simple, "Yes" then grabbed his hand turned it over and asked, "What's wrong with your wrist?"

"It has itched ever since they counted me with their machine."

"Counted you? Who counted you and with what?"

"Men dressed in black fatigues, they said everyone needed to be counted. They asked permission then ran a scanner thing over my wrist and told me to go. There was a man in front of me that didn't have any arms so they scanned his forehead." He mentioned with a weird little smirk.

"We have to get out of this city, now." I said trying to be calm, but knowing I was far from it.

"Someone told me they had blockades on every road that leads out of the city. I guess they won't let you leave unless they count you." Eanin stated without a conscience or care.

"You obviously have no idea what you agreed to when you let them mark you, did you?"

"What does it matter to you man? You act like I just killed someone."

"Guess your right it's not my eternity." I mumbled half out loud.

As the Jeep started rolling and those words left my tongue I receive a slap across the face from Malloy, literally. Then she told me what I had realized with the slap. "Have a little consideration. He didn't know."

"Know what?" finally interested in his predicament.

Malloy looked at me in a tone that said it all. "Never mind little brother, it's nothing."

The look of concern left his face as his sat back and then altogether lost interest as he stared out the window.

As swiftly as the insects had come, they were gone. I drove in silence as we maneuvered around the scattered crowd lying in the street displaying their agonizing pain. My mind contemplated situations yet to occur.

I did not know what it was going to take to get us out of that city. There was one thing on my mind I was certain of, we had to get out and I was not going to take the mark to do it.

Our way led northeast towards the outskirts of the city. The insects wounded many people we passed. Blood filled streets caused my heart to harden enabling myself to move on without stopping and helping.

The shroud of silence was broken when Malloy invited a feeble attempt of conversation when asking a question. "How far is it to your parent's house?"

"After we get out of the city it will take about two hours to reach our destination." Fully understanding the need to converse, I asked a question to keep it rolling. "Why hasn't Lex ever taken you out there?"

With a slight look of disappointment she answered, "We had made plans a few times, but you know how it is, something always came up."

"Yeah, some say there are just not enough hours in a day. If there were more we would just occupy them in the same way."

A smile brought a brilliant beauty to her face, which held my gaze for many moments, long enough to bring Eanin out of his paralyses state with a scream, "Rison!"

Slamming on the brake after seeing I was nearly off the road put my mind back on the track it should not had left.

Moments passed, spirits lightened as the end of our journey out of the city was presented. An exit, a butterfly, three sighs of relief came in that particular order just before our feeling of elation was quickly torn away.

Eanin had heard correctly. An impregnable blockade brought a sickness to my inner core and a thought of destruction to my mind. "Ram through it!" I told myself. Just before I hit the accelerator Malloy touched my arm.

"Don't do it, you will find a way" spoken softly from the lips of truth.

There was a vehicle in front of me. The men dressed in black were talking to him indistinctly. My mind knew the conversation-taking place.

"Sir, we simply can't let you pass without scanning you. Give me your left hand."

"I don't care" said the lonesome stranger "just do it but make it quick, I need to get out of this city."

The man reached in the car with his machine, pushed his button, milliseconds later the man in the car had a convulsive reaction that left a bad taste even in my mouth. The pain from the initial scanning was not a fear of mine; it was the eternal repercussion I feared.

The car moved forward, they made way, just before the employ of darkness stated his demand I hammered down on the accelerator leaving him spouting words in the distance.

The car in front of me did not move quickly enough so I helped him along with an aggressive nudge that put him sideways in the road. That reaction gave a blockade of my own and merited me a running start.

Jeeps are not speed demons by any means, yet they are maneuverable. It didn't take much to take out the few that perused. Soon after the minute chase we were anxiously on our way.

Not a thought of what lay ahead was spoken; we were too proud of our elusiveness to care. So, onward we traveled with smiles permeating on the corners of our mouths, fully knowing it was too good to be true but true none the less.

The more miles we put between that retched city and ourselves the better I felt. Though I knew with everything in me that our hardships had only begun, I was well enough to know they had subsided for the moment.

Miles passed with conversations of little meaning for my mind was elsewhere. I missed Fallon with every fiber that made me whole. Fallon had brought me life. Without her by my side I felt a slow decay, I was dying little by little as the moments passed. I wanted nothing more than to have her in my arms.

Within twenty miles of our destination a feeling crept over me. One I was sure was lost in the past due to the present. Oh how it is for one to slip into the past. Growing, life as a child without a care or a need any further than to be loved. Bright and beautiful are the dreams and desires of our youth. If only we as adults could hold on to it.

Familiar surroundings brought me closer to my home and brought thoughts of my childhood. The ones around me were quiet; quiet enough to let me turn these events over in my wavering mind. The smell of home entered my nostrils and a vivid picture of my family crashed into me.

Night was closing in on us as we arrived at my parents, where we were sure to find my brother. His vehicle was sure enough not visible and brought the moral to an all-time low.

Malloy stated the question that was obviously on all our minds, "Where is he?"

"Let's not lose our heads just yet," I said genuinely disgusted, "I promise you we will find him."

Surroundings brought back stains resonated in my memory inducing feelings of euphoria mingled in pain. It took not but a moment to see the house was vacant. Just as I had thought, my parents were taken in sweet slumber. Both sets of clothing in their sleeping positions set me back to the loss of which I tried to suppress but was likely not to ever forget.

By the time the inspection had been made the shadows completely lost themselves to full darkness. In my mind I knew fully of my brother's whereabouts.

Thirty miles east deeply covered in woods and solitude. I dare not speak of it. We needed rest and I had no call to journey any further till the earth shed some light on the situation.

Under starlight the night air was cool while nestled alone in the bed of my upbringing. My mind played torture on feelings of resent diabolical events. Tossing, turning, twisting my mind, at last I had enough. Sitting erect I lit a candle.

With help from a slow wind entering through a slightly cracked window the lights of the candle swayed. The shadow puppet that fell on the opposing wall sent me into a moment of paralysis. The image of a black horse and his rider whipped about, as the horse stomped his feet.

I returned to the darkness well enough alone and weary enough to fall from consciousness. That night I slept better than I had in years. Was it the exhaustion brought on by current events? Or was it simply being back in my old bed?

Morning came with a quickness and reluctance to get out of my resting place. Dim light filtered through the curtains making it hard to keep my eyes closed. After a good stretch and an even better crack of the neck I was willing to take on the day.

I crept about the house with minimal noise doing my best to make best of the situation. Coffee and breakfast was made bringing a pleasant aroma, also bringing life to the rest of the houses occupants. Even though I had ones beside me I had not ever felt more alone. Remembering times of resent past, cooking for the one I loved. How often do we take for granted simple pleasures that make us whole? Why do we not see them until they are not there to be seen?

Silence was the topic of conversation for I did not have it in me to entertain. As the meal ended so did my compassion for company, I needed time alone to think. A simple moment to relax, relax and think. What better place for such needs, than the comfort and caress of flowing water? So, to the lavatory I went.

I don't even remember taking off my attire; I think it just fell off. My mind searched for answers as my body drank deeply. By the end of my session the air lay heavy with condensation making beads on my forehead. When I reached for a towel and passed in front of the mirror I saw it. Maybe not as plain as day but I saw it, one word, cabin.

Not distinct but distinguishable, left by the fog hanging to the mirror my brother gave clue. Leave it to him to do just that. In that instant I knew my previous intuition was true and exactly what to do. To be furtive was of great importance so I made no attempt to fire from the lip as soon as this message was obtained. I wiped the mirror and continued with my duties.

I wanted to relieve their worried minds, yet that I could not do. Lexter had good reputation and reason for being stealthy. So silent I was.

The others were busy with themselves, giving me time to make ready the Jeep with spare gas and other novelties in my father's garage.

I had just finished packing and loading a minuscule amount of supplies when the silence was abruptly interrupted. Questions came and passed faster than they had time to completely dissipate from the air. I turned on my heel in one motion holding a momentary gaze answering all their questions with my look.

They were loaded into the Jeep before I had time to take one singular step in its direction. Not another word escaped from anyone until we pulled out of the garage.

The wind stirred nefariously instilling thoughts that should not be. An unspeakable evil fell upon us like a blanket of insanity invoking devilry. We all began to shout at one another with animosity and force. Words spewed from our mouths piercing one another with accuracy. The dark wind slowed . . . so did our words. Explanations for our actions were beyond our languages ability. Sickness overwhelmed and unconsciousness consumed.

We lay as if dead, for time was unknown. My eyes opened to a man of death upon a pale horse.

With those moments of unexplained uncertainty rang truth to the end of all things. I drove in darkened silence for Malloy and Eanin had yet to waken from their shadows of slumber. A brief duration passed with one singular thought . . . the desire to have done something different with time before time had been taken. My demise felt uncomfortably close. I could all but taste it.

My parent's house was lost from rear view, in the folds of land passed by, when my companions rose. Slow in speech but quick to question they held in common. I answered best I could as miles were put behind us.

The sun shone bright bringing warmth into the Jeep. Eanin rolled down his window giving us all a cool taste of country air. Periodically he dug his fingernails into his wrist shaking his head with a sour face. Malloy sat quiet while fidgeting with unknown objects from the glove box. Paved road turned to dirt, dirt turned to grass as our way was made to our desired destination.

After twists, turns, and an imminent descent into a large valley the cabin came into view. A sudden change of behavior fell over the brother and sister. Lexter had told Malloy about this place, I learned, as she told Eanin what she knew.

The cabin came in full view. When it did Malloy burst into tears startling Eanin and myself. Before I could utter a single syllable she screamed his name. His vehicle was nowhere in sight but that fazed me none at all. I knew he was close, I could feel him.

Out of the heavily wooded area behind the cabin came the one we had hunted. When Malloy cleared her sight with the swipe of her hand their eyes met.

Before I could stop the Jeep she had jumped out to hastily make her way to him. Their reuniting was one to hold close to the heart for even I could feel the warmth of their love. It was not a time to dwindle on the thoughts of my loss but a time to enjoy their rekindling. It did not take long before I had to look away. I longed for a loving touch of my own . . . I knew it was too far-gone and would not come.

Chapter VI

Our refuge was one not known to many. Members of my family built the four-room cabin for one purpose alone, seclusion. There were no permanent residents. Periodically ones would use that place just to get away from the monotony of everyday life.

The supplies Lex and I brought added to the provisions already stored in the cabin would enable us to survive for a few months. So, the first couple days lingered with getting comfortable in our situation and catching up on how this came to pass.

Mid morning on the third day Lexter and I lounged on the front porch speaking of old times as Malloy listened intently smiling all the while. Eanin busied himself down in the lower field with objects of no importance. The sun shined bright making my skin warm to the touch as the wind stirred an aroma sweet to smell. All seemed too good to last long and last long it did not.

Everything in those moments that brought feelings of comfort was lost when we heard a wretched scream from the lower field. In an instant we were all on our feet running towards Eanin. We had made it part way down the hill in front of the cabin when Eanin began to point behind us. We stopped and in one motion turned to witness what caused his dismay. With fire and force a large meteoric object raced across the sky. I had heard of only a few instances of a meteor of that size making contact with the ground and here we were observing it too close for comfort. Falling in our direction, just over the cabin, over us and ultimately landing in the forest far beyond the tree line that faced the cabin.

Trees began to fold in our direction like blades of grass being manipulated by ones hand. We started to run . . . we had no time. In one swift motion we were all taken from our standing positions.

The moment I hit by body half rolled half slide landing me on my back still able to see in the blasts direction. Craning my neck partly, I endured the sound of the contact. A euphemism would not give the sound justice.

All eyes fell on black smoke, resembling the black of a starless night, filtering to the sky above. We were in a state of awe, except for our curious of cats Eanin. He started to run as if he were going for a close inspection of the situation despite the commands from Malloy to stop.

For myself I would have let him go in hopes of ridding our selves of such foolishness. Lexter must have felt he had an obligation to control the matter because he put dirt and speed beneath his heals to bulldog him to the ground. He looked to Malloy for permission to continue and she gave consent. "What is wrong with you boy? Have you no sense?" said with a violent shake.

With hurt feelings and bruised body Eanin gave try. "I thought it would be alright if I just . . ."

"From this time forward you are not allowed to think," cutting him off with a serious tone of conviction. "Tell you what little man, before you take any action of any sort you will ask first. Do you understand?"

With a shrug of a shoulder he mumbled, "Yeah sure."

Lex slapped him loud enough to make my eye twitch and the boy reiterated with a, "Yes!"

I tried not to look upon this scolding lightly or directly. This boy was going to be more trouble than I was willing to put up with. He was blinded by his own will. Many fall to the resolve of saving others and I knew with everything in me that Eanin was beyond being saved.

The conversation had taken our attention when it should have been on the blackening sky. The smoke was slowly snuffing out our bright shining day. It seemed uncomfortably familiar, too familiar to ignore. My eyes watched close making sure the smoke was in fact smoke not locust making their way for us.

As a whole we made our way for the cabin. With each step the sky darkened, with each breath it darkened still. Being the last to go inside I turned around to have one more look before closing the door. Smoke had consumed light leaving all just as dark as life had left us. A low rumble grew in the darkness creeping its way into my heart and mind. Flashes of light gave momentary view of our grim surroundings. I stared out of the window for an uncalculated amount of time waiting for the locust to come.

Noises from above continued. My hypnotic gaze reached far beyond our world with a fool's hope of regaining comfort. My body ached with unfamiliar pains and all other senses dulled to a haze. Life was passing me by. The final moment had arrived, just before I took the great plunge into shadows I saw her face smiling back at me. Her smile breathed life back in my bones giving me reason to be. The more I wanted to stay in that moment the more it faded. Hard to understand or believe life had left me standing alone. I took a vow unto her, "Until death do us part."

Not ever did I fathom the thought of life parting us to exist on different planes. I searched for death in those moments of misery but death would not have me. On the swift wings of shadows death fled where I could not follow leaving me to deal with the life chosen.

Days turned to weeks as our "existence" gave meaning to the word. Our provisions held strong giving us one less obstacle, yet, we knew they would not last. Lex and I set live traps periodically escaping dinner from a can. We spoke of big game yet dare not chance the sound of a riffle alerting anyone of our safe haven.

Lex and I had many physical characteristics that made us look the same like broad shoulders, height, and muscles seeming to stand on the bone but there was more. The more we spent time together the more our actions and thought patterns were on the same level. Malloy even called me by his name a few times when we were standing a few feet apart while conversing. Cut from the same stone.

Malloy and Eanin on the other hand were from different substances entirely. Malloy looked as if she just stepped of the cover of your favorite magazine and when she spoke, had something to say. I was told by an elder with wisdom that one with wisdom speaks when they have something to say and a fool will speak because they think they have to. Eanin, short for his age and battling a serious case of acne spoke just to hear himself. I was sure they were not blood but was told otherwise by all three.

A cool breath of air had just escaped my lungs on that brisk autumn morning when Lexter mentioned a situation I knew was near. We need supplies to make it through the upcoming winter.

Winters were quiet mild in Central America, most of the time. Lex and I had the insatiable need for being prepared and if that meant going into town then into town we would go. I wouldn't say I had a bad feeling about it, I simply knew we were crossing the line.

Arguments were made when the decision came. I was going to town alone. We could not leave Malloy and Eanin at the cabin for the worry of happenstance and I did not trust Eanin in public. After making a list, my way was made ready.

The nearest town lay twenty miles towards the east. Money with list in hand I headed to the door. Lex reached out a deft hand to turn me around by my shoulder and spoke audaciously, "If you have not returned by nightfall I will come looking for you."

With a half smile and a full wink I told him I was not going to take more than a few hours.

"Just watch yourself and your back trail little brother."

As one being we gave each other a familiar look and gesture. After doing so the understanding resonated within me, we were both on the level.

I found my way on roads I hadn't traveled in years focused on the fact I was on a solo mission. This mission would enable us to live the winter through, which thought brought comfort.

After the third day at the cabin when the meteor fell with flame causing the sky to blacken with its destruction the sun had not regained full strength. What I mean is it didn't shine with the intensity it had before, though it was bright enough to need the use of my sun visor.

"Watch your back trail little brother," rang in my head with conviction.

Adjusting my rearview mirror I noticed something amiss. Not someone following me or what one would expect in those days like the earth opening up to eat me whole but this was something far beyond reason. Hiding in the back floorboard, almost covered by a blanket lie Eanin.

Blood ran cold in my veins. I wanted nothing more than to pull the vehicle over and beat him within a breath of lost life. Just as I started to break I passed an Envoy with blacked out windows. Normally it would have bothered me none at all, this vehicle locked its tires spinning sideways in the road. Cold blood boiled over, with second nature as instinct reaction was quick and precise. My vehicle was a prodigy of gumption for it didn't skip a beat.

I pulled Eanin by the scruff of his neck to the front seat and told him to buckle up with quickness. Eyes wide with fright he complied. We were on a mile straightaway giving the opposing vehicle gain, slightly. I worried not for I knew these back roads as well as the depths of my mind. Cutting through an intersection the road rapidly descended followed by a series of curves.

The Envoy was not in our view when we turned off the road taking a detour known by few. My breaths slowed, my mind raced and loosening my grip my knuckles returned to their normal color.

I wanted to take him back not only to rid myself of his insolence but also to relieve Lex and Malloy's minds. The persons in our pursuit were sure to figure out our maneuver and I knew we were too close to the town of Hector to turn around. I was stuck with him and it set my blood to boiling.

Displaced aggression has no place in my live so I put it in its proper place. A partially clenched fist into ones stomach will generally teach a lesson. The sound escaping from his lungs told me he understood with clarity.

Time pressed on bringing with it the limit of town. With his head hung low Eanin must have been thinking hard of his discernments and well enough he should have.

In the past I had visited the town of Hector but not ever had it looked so desolate. What should have been citizens busying themselves with daily activities was instead lost souls lurking in the shadows waiting for the sky to fall. I cared not that most businesses we past were lifeless. My only concern was obtaining our much-needed supplies and leaving the town to devour itself as it saw fit.

Relief turned quickly to distress when we arrived at the grocery store. Not a vehicle parked in the lot or a single strand of filament burning giving light to its inner working. Curiosity pulled us close enough to the entrance to notice a piece of paper hanging on the door. Before I could stop Eanin displayed his premature instincts by jumping out and running to read. The paper gave a new location-restoring moral to a respectable level.

I knew little of the warehouse side of town but specific directions were given and that is all I needed. The further we drove the more we saw the towns' inhibitors making their selves noticeable. Hector gave me an uneasy feeling. If it could have been explained I would have told myself the sense was all my own doing. Eanin felt it as well. I had no call to dwell long enough to figure out what caused everyone to subside as if they were waiting for a beating from their master.

"In and out." I repeated in my mind more often than it rolled of my tongue. Overhearing my blunt phrase I noticed Eanin agreed fully because he started repeating it too. Louder, louder, yet louder still we as one unit spat the phrase until we were screaming it to our greatest ability. Ultimately out of breath we were, but not so much to stop us from laughter of hideous proportion.

Our destination presented itself just about the time I started my demands of Eanin. "I only going to say this once so you better listen well. You are to stay by my side step by step while we gather the goods. Your mouth need do nothing more than breathe. If you defy me one iota" raising my fist to accentuate the meaning, "I will make you wish life had left your bones to rest far before we've met."

In a muffled tone I heard, "I'm not a little baby."

Doing my best to hold composure I balled my fist and slugged him on the top of his knee with more force than I should have. I really thought the boy was going to flop right out of the Jeep the way he was convulsing. "Alright man, whatever!" He said with a clenched jaw surely wishing my ears were not as keen as they were.

A bit of a smile arose at the opposing corner of my mouth with the thought of my malicious act serving two purposes. One, his realization I was not going to take his antics and knowing I spoiled any plans he had of running off due to his bum leg.

List in hand, boy by my side, we entered the enormous warehouse with our game faces on. I tried to suppress any negative thoughts pertaining to the possibilities of not obtaining my goal.

My first glance of the warehouse's interior brought a sense of euphoria for my eyes fell upon isles upon isles of surplus.

The store was by no means overrun with shoppers that particular day, but cliental there were. I felt at ease gathering the necessary items making hast, yet, doing our best to not look as if we were in a hurry. Eanin surprised me with his demeanor, it was the first time we were together I actually enjoyed his presents.

Each and every item on the list was found and placed in our overly filled cart. There were two registers unoccupied; I strolled into the closest one. Eanin gave me no reason to even raise an eyebrow; he became my shadow allowing a single thread of trust for him to develop . . . or bestow ever-creeping moments of vulnerability.

The man running the register had a familiar look about him, he smiled and I remember him faintly. Before a word was exchanged I pulled my wallet from my pocket and his look turned to unmistakable terror.

"Is something wrong?" I asked in a monotone voice.

"Rison, didn't ya know . . . they replaced the almighty dollar." He mentioned in a tone even lower than mine.

Keeping the tone going I gave question, "Who replaced it with what and how do you know me?"

"Have ya not been scanned, wow where the heck ya been?" He spoke secretly half covering his mouth.

"If it's all the same to you we'll let that be my own, now tell me how you know my name."

"There's no time for explanations ya need to get out of here bud, they're always watchin'."

"We need all of this" pointing to my cart "to make it through the winter."

"I can help ya if ya help me, meet me at the back of the warehouse in ten minutes, and now go." After his statement he turned on his heel so I followed suit.

A bolt of energy raced down my spine when I noticed Eanin was not behind me. Rounding a display gave me full view of the exit and the relief of seeing him waiting by the door.

I paid no attention to my ten-minute marker but surrendered my full attention to the task at hand. Eanin ask no questions, raising some of my own, during our fast pace trek to the Jeep.

Our arrival was premature but the cashier must have anticipated for he appeared and we pulled in his motioned direction through an opened garage door. I was uneasy about the stealthy operation but would have been much more uneasy without our supplies.

The door closed behind us leaving us in the pitch of black. Only a few seconds passed when the gift of light was given.

There stood the man, several full grocery sacks, and a young lady. My mind was made that I was leaving with those good no matter what.

Eanin and I jumped out of the Jeep leading the loading process to ease with quickness. The look on my face told the man it was time to explain, explain in short he did.

"As I said 'I'ma helpin' ya, so you help me', well here ya go. Take the all this and return for more only if ya'll take my niece with ya."

Giving respect to his bluntness I kept it simple, "Why and how can you trust us with her?"

"She is not safe here and I'ma trustin' ya 'cause I trusted your father Neol."

There was not much else to discuss, it was reason enough for me. We three loaded into the jeep as our helper opened our exit.

"Lay down in the floor board Roo, ya can't let anyone see you leaving." With a forced smile and a lonesome tear rolling down his cheek his final farewell was a partially raised hand.

Our departure set heavy within my heart and mind. Total apathy for their separation tore at what was left of my inner being. Lost love is hard to deal with; knowing a loved one exists but being separated by an impossible situation will drive one to a level of insanity far beyond comprehension.

While driving I moved my rear view mirror to get a better look at our-stow away. She was a fair skinned girl in her early twenties with curly dark hair accentuated with large strands of bright pink coloring. I spoke soft encouraging words of our destination and ensured her safety. My words were mostly unheard for she was far too busy nervously biting her black painted fingernails.

Eanin took an interest in Roo from the start. I don't know how many times he had to be told to turn around and not look at her directly. I minded not he was trying to become acquainted; I was only being as discrete as possible.

With a scoff and sour face I knew he didn't understand. I had full understanding of his actions when Eanin called me on mine.

Her soft features were easy on the eyes and the way she looked at me caused confusion making me turn the rearview to its original position. Suppressing unneeded thoughts we made for the back roads, I with a clear mind and clear back trail for us all.

I had no call to encounter the ominous Envoy or its occupants so my eyes constantly scanned the horizon. My anxiety subsided greatly when we enter the unbeaten path and diminished completely with view of the cabin.

The journey took longer than expected but was quickly put out of Lex and Malloy's mind as soon as they got hold of Eanin. He told of my abuse, it mattered little when Lex displayed his version of punishment.

They were so involved with Eanin that Roo's exit from the Jeep had gone unnoticed. Lex shook Eanin hard enough to release objects from his jacket. When a new pocket-knife, two bags of candy and a slick pair of eyeshades hit the ground questions hit the air.

Roo receded back to the Jeep knowing the situation was going to get worse as I did just the opposite.

Malloy was the first to speak, "Little brother, tell me you didn't steal this."

Before he could answer Lex step forward with his accusation, "You dirty little thief."

"Give him a chance Lexter." Malloy said displaying her benefit of doubt.

"I paid for it," receiving my comment of money being obsolete he retorted with one word, "honest."

As one voice we three shouted, "How!"

"With my wrist thing, I overheard Rison and that dude talking so I went to talk to the lady on the other register."

Rubbing his wrist he continued, "I asked how people paid for stuff. She told me that everyone that's been scanned is put in this giant computer thing and given an account." With a proud little smug look on his face he boasted, "They gave everyone who did it one hundred dollars for free, so ha!"

An eerie silence fell over us while we let his confession resonate. Malloy started to comment but her oppression clearly stopped the words from exiting her mouth.

Lex flinched, obviously startled by Roo stepping out from behind the Jeep. He instantly looked to me for enlightenment.

I had not the energy to edify, just before I mustered the strength Roo spoke, "I'm cold. May I go in the house?"

"Sure doll, go on in and make you comfortable. Malloy, Eanin, if you would be so kind would you grab a couple bags and show her around, we will be in shortly."

As they were retrieving the bags Roo glided to me, softly put her hand on my shoulder and said, "My uncle belongs to a secret alliance, I overheard their meetings. Let me get cleaned up and something to eat and I will be happy to tell you what I know." Her voice made me a little tense. I was not sure if it was apprehension or her sensual tone.

She followed the others to the cabin and Lex told me exactly what I was thinking. "Little brother, that little chick has a thing for you; you best better watch your pints and quarts around her."

"Will do mister. That little lady knows exactly what she's doing." I was doing my best to advert my eyes from watching her walk away.

We pulled the rest of the supplies from the Jeep while I told my brother the details of our trip. He mostly listened with an occasional nod or grunt. Essentially he agreed with the way I handled the whole situation and told me he would have done the same. After storing our goods I was ready to relax and aid the call of a cup of coffee.

Malloy and Roo were close enough to the same size helping Roo with her clothing dilemma. We all roamed around the cabin doing whatever we needed to do to make ourselves comfortable. With full stomachs and lounge attire we waited for Roo to finish her shower. Conversation weaved through the moments of silence just enough to hold our trepidation.

Dressed in clothing that hid her features Roo entered the room designed for living and released her prelude. "I don't have all the answers but what I have overheard has been passed through ones whom have seen firsthand and can be trusted till death. Organization unknown to society has anticipated the coming for a time uncalculated. There is a diabolic group designed for a singular purpose, their purpose is eternal destruction and the time draws near."

Her words made us all shift uneasily in our seats. Gliding with grace she sat herself in a chair facing us all. She looked directly into my eyes giving me a sensation I had not felt in quite some time. The thought dissipated rapidly and I nearly bit a hole in my tongue as rare form took control of my body.

"My uncle Charles took the mark with full knowledge of its repercussions because he was willing to sacrifice his self for those he could save. Being marked he is not looked upon as a threat giving him the chance to obtain certain information to pass on to those whom the B.E.A.S.T. seek."

With no recollection of who ask the question still the question rang like a Sanctus Bell. "What's the BEAST?"

"The people in the secret society say they are the Bureau Extirpating All Sanguine Tenders."

Eanins reservation depleted mustering his question. "What the heck does that mean?"

"Uncle Charles said they are those whom seek all people resisting the stain."

On the edge of her seat with concern Malloy asked, "Stain?"

"Yes, the eternal blood stain, and the one I'm sure you all have unavoidably denied."

"What does it matter if someone wants to get marked or not? Is this not a free country?" Lex mentioned obviously disturbed as Eanin buried his face in a pillow.

"Millions of people just vanished in thin air, important people. They say even the President disappeared right in front of the First Lady and most of his staff during breakfast. They had to initiate some sort of order and have a way to keep track of those still present."

Roo gave us not a single moment to speak though I know we all had plenty to say. She carried on for quite some time about speculations brought forth by her uncle on possible future events. After a few minutes of letting her stray from the important points I finally cut her off with a question that could no longer wait.

"Roo, what are they doing to those who won't take the mark?"

"Oh, that is exactly why Uncle sent me away. They are putting all those resisters into prison."

In disbelief I replied, "Now, the news is always complaining how prisons are too crowded anyway, please explain."

With a glare only a twenty year old could perform as she through her hands in the air and responded, "Every convict that complied with the Bureau were released. Why do you think the cities are being overtaken by havoc and people in small towns like Hector are scared to even go outside?"

Blinking a few times to alleviate my stare I gave a nod in understanding. The others seemed to all start talking at once making it hard for me to think.

With a solitary hand raised Roo spoke her final words for the evening. "Listen everyone; I told you from the start, I don't have all the answers. I have grown weary from today's toils. We will talk tomorrow, where can I sleep?" Malloy led her to her room with haste, then returned quickly as well.

"Eanin, why don't you retire to your room little buddy, Rison and I need to talk." After Lex's request Malloy took Eanin by the arm and they began to exit.

With squinted eyes speaking under his breath as usual Eanin began to comment on the fact of being too old to be sent to his room. To his room he went dragging his feet every step of the way.

Interest held me in a most particular way while waiting for Eanin to fall from earshot and Lexter to begin. Lex started to speak then started to act paranoid.

He began by moving closer soon followed by series of looking around thoroughly making absolutely positive we were alone. My interest turned quickly to concern watching him act so discreet.

"Listen little brother, you know I'm not the kind of guy to talk about this sort of thing. I have to say something, it's eating me up." My silence and full attention he had during continuation. "I've had a reoccurring dream far more vivid than any dream I have ever had. Now, you know more than anyone I don't believe in dreams coming true but parts of this one has."

I was not sure whether he paused hoping I wouldn't make fun or needing a boost of reassurance. I gave him the latter. "I also have had my share of significant dreams lately. Go ahead Lex do tell."

"I dare not tell it in its entirety 'cause it involves you, negatively. Anyway, the night before you three showed up I dreamed you did. It came true, detailed to the tee. Down to the clothes you were wearing. Other stuff too, like that girl," saying with a thumb jerked in her direction, "not her face exactly but it was her no doubt."

He was fidgeting in an unfitting manner causing me to wonder about the information he was not letting go of. I started several time during his conversation to ask but the way he acted I wasn't sure I wanted to know.

Calming down to a respectable degree by some comforting words made me feel better as well. His brain was working overtime; I cut him off just as he started to initiate further talk on the matter. "Hey man, I am somnolent; if I'm not careful I might not make it to my bed."

Standing feebly I took a few steps in the room's direction biding him a good night. I received no feedback. Turning to face him I caught a look I was well familiar with.

He was displaying his version of disappointment. I took his demeanor into quick consideration and mention the one thing I knew would raise his spirit. "Tomorrow, we will take those old bows you found in the basement out to the woods and hunt."

Chapter VII

The next morning was brought with quickness and surprise. Snow lay heavy on everything in its reach. Lex and I were conditioned in hard ways so the snow bothered us in the least. Suddenly a scream shrieked out springing us both into immediate action.

Instantly we arrived at the origin of the disturbance. Sitting by the bathroom door rocking back and forth holding his right eye was Eanin. Lex turned his head enough for me to notice his smirk speaking out of the corner of his mouth. "What did you get yourself into this time little fella?"

Bursting to his feet quicker than I had ever seen him move he shout, "Just shut up, I didn't know she was in there!"

When those words had only reached the tip of his tongue the bathroom door swung open nearly dislocating from its hinges. Eanin wasted no time in his retreat while Roo reassured him of being a pervert and a liar.

We did our best not to chuckle during her convincing statement and I found it hard to listen for I was too busy adverting my eyes and my mind's eye from her wrapped in a towel. She noted our demeanors as being unfit for the serious situation in a stomping display to her room. In a mirrored image of one another Lex and I shrugged our shoulders spit a sigh/laugh and returned to our previous duties.

With full stomachs and necessary equipment packed we set out for a morning hunt. The girls waved happily while Eanin showed a crude gesture for his goodbye.

The cold was unforgivable. Energy levels were low due to our lack of protein, hence the hunt. By mid-morning we found our marksmanship abilities had not depleted in years passed without practice. Small talk of how we were going to prepare the three rabbits made my mouth water profusely.

When the sun found itself high in the sky looking directly down on us we found a reason to be excited. Evidence of large venison was given by fresh tracks in the snow. The teachings of our father spoke out from beyond guiding stealthy movement insuring the ability to succeed.

44

Lex picked up his pace and began a wide flanking maneuver as I slowed giving him ample time. No sooner did I lose sight of its tracks than did I find them simply by keeping to their trajectory.

A white flicker grasped my immediate attention. My breath slowed, my heart sped during my visual search for Lexter. His presents was made and not a moment too soon. The deer caught sight of Lex sending the young buck in my direction. Imitating stone I stood, arrow notched, bow fully drawn I waited. The buck was so intent on evading my brother he failed to notice me. His haste gave me all the chance I needed, not more than twenty feet separated us for my picture perfect broadside shot. With a relaxed exhale I released. The hit was true, yet, vital it was not.

Lexter took no time finding me in my intent search for the blood trail. For being seriously injured the buck sure put yardage under his hooves.

I held tenacious while Lex began to show signs of fatigue and disinterest. With first mention of giving up, I told him to head on back I needed a little more time.

With the rabbits in his pack and my assurance of being along soon, our separation began. The blood trail nearly thinned to nothing at the time he crossed my field of vision.

Elated to the point of clumsiness, I stumbled my way to the day's prize. Quickly kneeling by his side, I gave thanks for trading his life for my nourishment.

Taking the best cuts and filling my pack to the point of congestion I left the rest to nature. A smile permeated my face creating a bit of skip in my step. The gesture grew larger with the thought of all the others having the chance to enjoy the meat too.

Staring through the timber into an opening I distrusted my eyes in hopes they were deceiving me. Crouching down slowly my gaze became fixed on a lone stranger straddling a pale horse. His movements told me he was looking for something or someone. I had the distinct feeling he was a member of the Bureau searching for ones of my nature.

My movements were minimal as I blended with my surroundings. The scout did not notice me for he moved on slowly leading away from the cabin's direction. Soon after he fell from sight I progressed closer to my goal.

The sun retreated behind the hills moments before I entered the lower field. Fully clothed, heading in my direction, Lex released a sigh of relief when he saw me. With his index finger aimed at me he began to scold, "You know better than to cut it this close to dark, I was worried!" Those last three words merited me a slug in the arm making a tingling sensation run a course throughout.

"Did not mean to cause grief mister, I have good reason for my tardiness. First things first, take this." Handing over the pack of meat we departed to the cabin.

The girls were excited to see we had fresh meat enter the house. With no hesitation they began cleaning the venison methodically. While they busied themselves Lex and I invented a makeshift instrument for allowing the meat to drain excess blood.

All four working as a unit made the task a simple one indeed. Something was amiss or better put, missing. With the process of elimination the answer was quickly found. Eanin was not among us which didn't fit anywhere in the picture. He was always right in the middle doing his best to be noticed.

Mentioning my thoughts on the matter Malloy told of his reclusive behavior being an all day event. Asking her to further investigate the situation to ease my wonders she agreed to do so after doing a few more chores.

My body needed attention one can only receive from a shower. No better way to put the day behind one's self than to watch it swirl down the drain into nonexistence. I was putting the finishing touches on my self-maintenance when Roo burst through the door catching me unclothed.

With partially shielded eyes breathing sporadically she explained her intrusion with brevity. "There's something terribly wrong with Eanin, he feels like he's on fire and he is hardly breathing! Hurry up and help us!"

I have no recollection of dressing myself at all. The stain resonated in my memory holds only Roo's explanation then my arrival for assistance.

She exaggerated none at all; first glance showed he was fever stricken on the brink of mortal danger. Our inclement weather directed me to our only option.

Removing his attire, save his boxers, Lex and I hoisted him from his bed. Moving through the house as quickly as possible I studied him briefly. His unconsciousness kept him silent and his eyes were open revealing an inauspicious soul. We carried him out the front door placing him in the snow. In an instant he came to life. Lex and I held him as the girls used their hands to cover him in snow resisting all the while. His screams were forceful to the point of being muted. In short time his fight subsided, his muted screams turned to a low moan and we eased our hold.

Subsequent to our reentry to the cabin, Eanin was tightly wrapped in a blanket and positioned near the fireplace. Slowly walking away from him I heard him mutter two words, "She's mine." Speculations I had, concern I did not.

Weary were my muscles and feeble was my mind at the day's end. The knot in my stomach kept me from enjoying the fulfillment of food. The insatiable need for sleep weighed heavy causing me to be short when the others tried to converse. Lexter pointed out my attitude was of an impossible nature and I took it as my cue to vacate to the sanctuary of sleep.

When morning came around so did I. Tossing, turning, searching for a comfortable position I received only the will to become more restless. Indistinctly I heard animosity passing from the room adjacent to mine.

Curiosity mustered my energy an adequate amount to remove myself from bed. By the time I reached the door my need to know diminished along with the overheard conversation.

Stepping through on making way to appease a coffee craving I heard a faint sobbing from Roo.

I do not like having to be a mediator and I like turmoil even less. In an unobtrusive tone I offered my assistance. "Hey girlie, I'm going to have a cup of coffee and ready myself for a stroll. Would you like to join me?"

Wiping her tears with noticeable embarrassment she held her tongue but gave a forced smile and positive nod.

We exited the house unobserved. Inhaling the cold winter's air cleared my mind. Unzipping her coat I could see she was comfortable with the temperature. For a respectable amount of time we walked without a single word. We were obviously content with each other's reserve and company.

In the act of kindness she started our conversation with questions to better know me. I answered with an occasional question of my own. In a short time we knew each other's birthplace and date, favorite foods and hobbies. Many topics had little meaning but as a whole held great value.

I held one question for the better part of an hour then I couldn't help but ask. "Roo, is that your full name?"

She stopped abruptly squared herself with me and said, "My uncle gave me that nickname. My real name is Rosilyn Nichole." With a smile and a step we continued.

Past relationships were short lived in our talk for it pained me to speak of mine and to my surprise she had none to speak of. "What do you mean you have none to talk about? Surely one with those captivating eyes and the mind you posses love could be found around any corner." I mentioned with sincerity.

Again she stopped, so I turned and walk back stopping a few feet from her. "I have never been with a man before." She said with an innocence I have not ever witnessed.

Before I could comment on the matter she closed the gap between us, wrapped her arms around my neck and pressed her lips to mine.

Holding her shoulders tightly I pulled her away ever so gently, looked deep into her eyes and spoke with empathy. "Listen close sweet one, in time my heart will learn to love again. When that time comes you will be the one I look upon to complete those feelings. For now I must still mourn the love I've just lost. This is something I need you to not only understand but also help me with, please."

With a tear forming in the corner of her eye she agreed with a nod and lowering her head. Sensing she needed more than words I put a curled index finger under her chin raised it until we were eye to eye then kissed her with simplicity on the cheek. The smile on her face explained her understanding.

Rustling leaves in the distance grasp both of our attention. As one we quickly turned to find Eanin hiding poorly in the bushes eavesdropping. When he knew his cover was blown he cut and ran. I shouted his name hoping he would join us on our return to the cabin not quite understanding his evasiveness.

Roo slid her arm around my waist causing me to give her full interest. "I didn't tell you why I was so upset this morning. After seeing you the situation just disappeared." Displaying an odd look she continued. "Just before you came out of your room Eanin grabbed my arm and told me I was going to be his girl 'no matter what'." Silence held . . .

She rolled up her sleeve revealing three bruised marks resembling the shapes of fingers. With a cute little huff she finished, "This is what made me cry, not his immature display of stereotypical male ego."

An acrid taste formed in my mouth, my left eye twitched uncontrollably and my face flushed fire red with blood. A thought of inflicting pain beyond comprehendible reason kept me from instant movement.

Inspecting her arm extensively Roo paid me no mind, when she did speak my name in her monotone voice it extinguished the flame.

In those few moments I realized an important attribute of the one whom stood before me, humanity in pure form. A rarity it was and hard to believe. All good should have diminished with the coming, yet, here stood one as pure as spring's first rain. The nature of her voice brought a memory of Fallon rendering pain in my sternum.

Resembling a star fading in dawn's light her voice traveled to a place my ears could not follow. Reality struck conveying clarity to the words formulated by Roo. "You don't look so good Rison; I think we better go on back to the house."

Slightly embarrassed by my spell I could only muster a few words but it was just enough to move us in our direction home.

Clearing the heavily wooded path gave us a simultaneous view of the cabin and Lex running with full speed ultimately tackling an intruder. At the moment contact was made Roo let out a scream with full intentions of stopping Lexter. Before I could react to her scream I was already in motion to assist my brother.

Roo was not far behind when reaching a familiar man held tightly in Lexter's grip. I was too short of breath to spit out a word so I waved my arms signaling Lex to desist all actions as Roo fell to her knees, in the snow, embracing her Uncle Charles.

Lex stood erect looking mighty proud of his aggressive behavior as he brushed snow from his clothing but quickly changed his view with Malloy's disapproval.

Only a few moments passed before Charles assessed his contusions merely being superficial wounds. Less time passed before we found ourselves in the cabin waiting for him to clean up and enlighten us on his intrusion.

Sitting down, Charles had yet to fully recover for he nearly spilled the coffee he was holding while shaking uncontrollably. Roo didn't let but a few feet separate her from her uncle, before Charles became comfortable enough to pronounce a syllable she was parked on the arm of his chair. Whispering delicately in her ear she slowly walks over to the dining room retrieved a chair then sat beside him quietly.

His mouth started to open to speak but Lexter cut him off ever so rudely, yet, with understandable concern. "So, how is it you know of this cabin sir?" This was said with an obvious sarcastic tone meriting an elbow from Malloy. "What! He needs to tell how he knows."

Holding his side where Malloy elbowed him he continued, "We also need to know if he has told anyone." His question was quite reasonable and did need a thorough answer.

Clearing his throat he gave a little smirk and started his explanation, "You boys are just like your father was at that age, uncanny, let me tell ya. This will ease your minds, and then maybe you'll quit guarding me like dogs. I helped your father and grandparents build this here place."

At times I see myself as a cynic or skeptic, my brother outdoes me by far. Proving my point he blurted, "Give us one reason why we should believe you!"

Fatigue resonated heavily within the man but rise he did, with two words we were right behind him, "Follow me."

Leading us to the fireplace he looked directly at Lexter and asked him to look under the hardwood mantel for an inscription. Fulfilling his demand Lex took it a step further and started to read, "MAY WE ALWAYS FIND REFUGE . . . cutting him off abruptly with a powerful voice Charles finished the inscription holding his eyes to the ceiling, "IN OUR FRIENDS."

Stepping back a pace Lexter held out his hand stating, "Then friends you will have." They shook hands and everyone took a deep breath in relief.

"Now may I relax dear friends, I'ma hurtin' something awful?" Subsequent to his return to a chair he lifted his pant leg revealing a hideous sore far from disturbing.

Instantly Roo set into action with motion and words. Her uncle briefly held her at bay by telling her nothing could be done to alleviate or cure his ailment.

Not taking his words for an answer she hastily gathered supplies to clean the wound and wrap it properly. Charles caused no fuss while his niece went about those duties.

Noticing her brother was taking an alarmingly long time in the lavatory Malloy began to question through the door. Eanin assured her he was fine, he told her he just felt extra dirty, and not to worry.

When someone tells you not to worry about something that's about the time a person needs to start worrying.

Eanin must have forgotten to lock the door. With her insatiable concern for her brother's well being she investigated further. We all heard the door squeak on its hinges and Malloy shriek with terror. I sat still Lexter did not. He reached the door just in time to have it slammed in his face.

Obviously annoyed by their action Lex slugged the door with a closed fist. I was surprised he only released a low grunt not divulging a series of words to express his thought on the matter. He returned to his seat, dragging his feet all the way. Contemplating wonder without words we waited . . .

When I finally had enough of our silent game I broke ice with a question of simplicity. "Charles how's the warehouse?" I was doing my best to be convincing in a feeble attempt of being personable.

Seeing through my week point, yet, understanding my angle he played along. "Keeps me movin' like a hen on hot rocks but puts food on the table and . . . listen I have too much on my mind to make small talk. I need a bit to work this out in my head before I tell y'all. Hope ya understand."

Clasping a hand around the back of his neck he lowered his head in thought.

"No problem." I mentioned sharply. With a few moments of thought behind his comment I understood with consideration.

Lexter had gone down to the basement to vent off a bit of steam and returned with a surprise. His left hand was full of cigars; his right held an aged bottle of Spanish Rum. "Found a few novelty items, would anyone be interested?"

Charles beat Roo and me to the punch with a throat clearing gesture and a reach. After Lex recovered a few glasses from the cupboard we began to smoke and drink as if we were tainted youth.

Conversation held no water because our intentions were clear, smoke and drink resembling contaminated kids. With the thought of tainted youth a question shot from my lip, "Hey brother, they ever coming out of that bathroom?"

His first glance told me I didn't think the question over enough before asking. "Wouldn't care if they stayed in there all night." With his slur it was evident the drink was taking affect.

Each one of us found his comment humorous and displayed muffled laughter. Sending chills head to toe a voice materialized from dark, "Then maybe we will!" When Malloy said that I am almost positive we all levitated from our seats.

Subsequent to regaining our composure we watched Malloy and her little brother find their way into our drunken circle. When my eyes fell upon Eanin questions were answered as to their reclusion.

His attire consisted of shorts and a T-shirt. Much of his skin had burst open with loathsome sores causing him difficulty with movement. Malloy had a dark colored sheet and spread it on the chair he was to be seated in. With great intricacy he did his best to settle his body but the look on his face gave him away.

My first encounter with Eanin initiated my next action and his apparent ailment supported it. I took the remaining bottle of Rum directly to him telling him it was his to finish. Remarks around the room agreed with my decision.

Eanin began to consume, Charles reverted all eyes and attention to himself when he started his conversation. "Without even askin' little buddy I know you've got the mark," looking directly towards Eanin. "I know 'cause everybody with its acoming down with those sores like we've got." Taking a moment to drag his cigar he first filled the air with smoke, then with his next statement. "Hope y'all are ready for war." He said while coughing as he put the cigar back to his lips.

Lexter sat on the edge of his seat addressing the same issue on the tip of my tongue. "War! With who?"

"Settle down Logan, I've got a lot to tell, so be patient, I'll try to get it all out as quickly as I can bump my gums."

"No one's ever called me by that name except my father; you must have known him better than I thought."

"He and I started an assembly. A gatherin' of those willin' to stay behind and lead all those unstained people to safety." Clearing his throat with an uncomfortable movement he alleged, "Well, guess they just pulled rank on ol' Neil and took him in the first round up." The smile he had on his face was forced but sincere.

The volume of his voice influenced me in believing he was deep under the influence when Eanin asked the fate of those stained. Charles looked around wide-eyed in disbelief of our reservation. Charles wanted to come right out with the truth but Malloy made it a point to cut them off by telling Eanin he had drank too much and he needed to go to bed.

For the first time I had known him I felt proud once he jerked clear of Malloy's grip and demanded to be told the ramifications of his compliance.

Malloy stormed to her room after Charles told his little buddy that the pain he felt from his sores compared to the future pains as pleasure.

In a state of denial Eanin through the empty bottle of Rum across the room, nearly hitting me, and ultimately shattering against the opposing wall. Shortly following the silence of falling broken glass he exited the room as well.

Dark thoughts crowded my mind; 'If it weren't for that boy's sister he would have found his self-gagged, bound and alone deep in wooded hills. Maybe as the boy sleeps . . .' dissipating as quickly as they appeared my thoughts found reality and listened to Charles.

"Listen good boy's I won't be repeatin' this again. Them other two could get awful sore if they heard me so I gotta be quick. The bureau's lookin' for ya, all on the account of that youngster getting' scanned in the warehouse."

Doing his best to hold composure Lex inquired, "How would they know he was with us, unless that little brat opened his big mouth?"

"Hold your tongue 'till I'm finished, let me get this out." He didn't even wait for acknowledgement before he continued. "That group is a whole lot smarter than anyone knows, so you best stay clear of town. If anyone, I mean anyone comes snoopin' around you best not let 'em get away. If you know what I mean." He completed his comment with an index finger sliding from one ear to the other.

Brutal as it were he made more sense than we were willing to dispute. He let his words sink in for a moment, he said to two words before stopping, "Our alliance . . ."

Malloy had made her way to the kitchen causing Charles' abrupt silence. With a distrusting glance in her direction he planted the idea of sleep and we harvested before it even had time to grow.

If I had ever lost sleep over anyone it was that particular night I could refer. Eanin and his antics perpetuated constantly as I turned, tossed, grunted and growled. I had high hopes the Rum would have put me out quickly; it just was not enough.

As the sun rose so did I, there was not fight enough in me to stay in bed with my mind treating me the way it was. I made a round to assess the inhibitors. All were well within the realm of slumber save one, Charles.

He was to sleep on the couch in the living quarters. His blankets were neatly folded in a pile with a note residing on top. Rubbing my eyes briefly the letter read, Friends: Don't go worryin' on me we'll be seein' one another again soon.

P.S. Love Ya Roo,
Charles

Disturbed by his departure I was but letting it bother me little for the fish I had already caught were fighting the idea of being fried.

Chapter VIII

Dreams came and went as did the harsh days of winter. Roo and I grew closer than I had anticipated in those few months relative to Newton's third law. The closer Roo and I became further the distance became of Eanin. Oh how his ever-watchful eye made me uneasy at times. Malloy and Lexter were stone; they were perfect for each other. When one was down the other lifted, times were hard they worked harder to make it better. Really made me wonder what I would have done without them.

Small signs brought the anticipation of an early spring and with the purpose of preparation. Lex couldn't spend enough of his spare time pilfering through that crowded basement. I didn't ever complain because it came with good reason. In one of his searches he came upon seeds of various types, ones sure to insure enjoyable meals. Being as one with my brother there was no surprise when Malloy found a few eye-covered potatoes stowed away perfect for planting.

Before the time had come for planting the old rule "Don't work, don't eat" came into play. Taking turns, we manually plowed the lower field. Eanin did his part daily and daily he let us know his feelings on the matter. The rest of us went on through our daily tasks with the comfort of accomplishment as our gumption's fuel.

By the time we completed our first planting concern began to rise quicker than the potatoes. We were all standing in the lower field admiring our work when a small murder of crows flew overhead. With no apparent reason the magnitude of the murder fell to the ground, lifeless.

Eanin picked one up bringing the most disturbing fact to notion, "Hey look everyone their already stiff." With a laugh he tossed it aside searching for another.

Rigor mortis set in with the impact? The situation did not set well with the rest of us. We were unexplainably distressed to the point of pacification. I was confident it was just another implausible incident. I was the only one to blame for my predicament, taking it on one tragedy at a time was the only option. With those thoughts in mind and my exhausted body I turned in early. Hard work may be rigid on the body but there is no better way to receive a good night's sleep.

The early morning's light and the rumble of thunder brought me out of my much-needed slumber. I had no more than a cup of coffee in me before the sound of heavy rain set the mood.

With my second cup in hand I stretched out on the divan soon to be joined by Roo. She curled tightly by my side clearly seeking comfort of her own. Showing affection was in short order those days, I tried to appease but knew my actions lacked sincerity. She was a tenacious one I'll give her that. I did enjoy her to the fullest extent, just couldn't give myself away again knowing the ramifications of loss.

My eyes were resisting my will to keep them open. I had no need to make fight so I let them have their way. Roo and I barely moved during that day, doing well in losing itself to recuperation. Rain's best friends are rest and relaxation.

An eye opened with the distinct sound of a riffle hammer readying for fire, then came the percussion.

My hair stood on end as the bullet screamed by my ear splintering wood on the far wall. Abhorrent rage rapidly coursed through my veins raising adrenaline to an all time high. I sent Roo through the air sprawling as I came off the divan to face my opponent, Eanin.

His malicious stare turned quickly to fear in the clearing smoke as he noticed his mark was not true. Instantly he dropped the gun to the floor. I hurled the couch with full expectations of having to chase him down. His fear rendered him motionless except for his eyes. They grew larger as the space separating closed rapidly.

My arm sprang forward in a straight jabbing motion hitting my mark, directly in the throat. The hit stole his breath sending him flat on his back. My blows came quickly as his blood began to flow. I felt pressure of some sort on my back but I paid it no mind while I did my best to knock death into that vengeful being.

Before I was satisfied with his beating the pressure on my back increased to a strangle hold administered by my brother. Bending at the waist I catapulted him a few feet giving myself enough time to kick Eanin maliciously in the gut. My aggression was sufficed seeing my thrust didn't move him; he was out cold.

Lex made no effort to further restrain me as he noticed I was through. I stood still and did blink once while watching for his chest to rise with breath . . . there was none.

Malloy must have been unavoidably detained previous to the moment watching her presence become accentuated with a wailing cry. Finding no vitals Lexter began C.P.R. I was unbothered by the thought of his death, rather elated.

His life returned with his first breath. Lexter backed away giving me a look of full understanding. Malloy took Lex's place on the floor cradling her little brother in her lap. Her sharp look made me stand a little straighter. She started to speak but was instantly suffocated by my statement.

"Don't think for a second I will listen to a signal word signifying I'm the one at fault." Her look supported a sympathetic statement was next, in Eanin's defense, also suffocated. "He knew exactly what he was doing and you know it! Just sit there and be thankful he's not dead even though he deserves to be."

Clinching my teeth while feeling my temples throb intensely I quickly grew sick of the acrid smell of smoke and the sight of my nemesis. Without further thought I exited the cabin, alone. Long moments grew whereas the weather cultivated strength, as did my detestation for Eanin.

Standing and watching simply did not suffice my need for cleansing instigating my actions. Slowly, I walked to the lower field conscious of every raindrop and its contact. The crash of thunder reminded me of Eanin's attempt, his image flashed with every lightning strike. Diabolic thoughts suffocated my sanity.

When reaching the bottom an old oak tree presented sanctuary. First sitting then lying on my back, with closed eyes, I let go of realities bitterness. Listening to rain rustle leaves, splatter on the ground and collect into puddles brought tranquility. Aggression's flame grew dim and I could breathe again.

I inhaled deeply when her warm lips touched mine.

She stood in silence . . . I had no words. With my back against the tree I watched Roo's silhouette glide towards me. A short flash of lightning interrupted the darkness, briefly revealing her uncovered flesh. She found her way back to me and I found no reason to resist.

Rain washed over our bodies as light exploded periodically illuminating love in rare form. Death could have taken me then for I was sure life had no greater feeling than those moments possessed.

Small portions of the sky gave clear view to stars brighter than they had been in some time. We held each other with love's intensity resisting the urge to end our night. When the time had come to return to the cabin we both acted as one being.

A simultaneous sigh showed our relief in finding the house in silence and the occupants shut away in their rooms. On the tips of our toes we moved towards our ascribed rooms. Just before we parted we gave each other a look that said it all. I walked through the door to my room, took a small side step allowing her to pass, and then I secured the door from the rest of the house.

Under illume our bodies were woven tightly radiating warmth and manner. It was evident we needed each other and being a perfect match was more palpable still. Just before my mind fell beyond awareness Roo spoke, "The world will change, my feelings for you will remain. You have my heart Rison; do with it what you will."

My hold became a degree tighter telling her, "I will hold it as I am holding you now, firm and close to my own."

Our words resonated within before sleep took us.

We wanted Lexter and Malloy to know our situation as soon as we could. Before I had a chance to finish the first sentence they stopped me. "We saw it the first day she arrived by the way you to have looked at each other." Lex mentioned and Malloy shaking her head with every word.

"What are we going to do about Eanin?" Obviously concerned, Roo continued, "We were just sleeping on the couch, what's he going to do when he finds this out?" She had my hand in a death grip when directing her question towards Malloy.

"I don't think you'll have to worry about my little brother getting out of bed for quite a while." I was relieved that she looked in his bedroom's direction during that statement instead of straight at me.

Doing my best of faking concern I asked, "Is he going to be alright?"

"Sure, he'll come out of it. Being beat up this bad is a first but not the first time he's been beat up. Somehow I always get stuck taking care of him." The sound of her voice told a story of a big sister tired of helping a little brother whom refuses to grow up.

Reaching out and patting her shoulder I told her with sincerity, "If I can assist you in any way please let me know."

Looking at me as if I had done enough already she agreed to do so. We all knew better though.

Passing by his bedroom door I stole a glance. His sister exaggerated none at all. His face was swollen; his breathing irregular and a low groan accentuated his predicament. I came close to feeling bad for the boy, close.

Several weeks passed putting far beyond what should have been spring in full blossom. It was not as to be expected. Nut baring and fruit baring trees refused to produce leaves. Only the eldest of the other species showed life. Blue grass had once resided but was replaced by patches of Bermuda and even larger patches of thistle weed.

The overall look of foliage lowered our hopes for a productive garden. Some seeds we planted gave promising growth others were certain failure. Potatoes, carrots and beats gave a positive indication of producing. Tomatoes, green beans, bell peppers and cucumbers gave no sign of even being planted.

My mouth watered, oh how it yearned for the sweet taste of tomatoes and cucumbers. The buds on my tongue desired, moreover, demanded their thirst be adequately rewarded for the planting. I wanted nothing more than to appease each and every one of them or at least assure them it would be soon but it was not within me to be of illusion.

Knowing I was distressed by the plant's defiance to generate Roo knelt in the dirt by my side, touched my hand and told me what I needed to hear. "Lover, if you long for something sweet just say so." My face gave a surprising look; she melted me with a radiant smile and gave me a kiss.

Attention reverted to those giving substantial growth and displaced the others somewhere within our minds.

She was correct; I was focused on loss instead of on what was really important.

How often in everyday life do we become so involved in the search for enjoyment that we neglect the very nature of our existence?

When Roo and I found our way to the cabin night had found its way of settling in. Readying myself for supper I noticed a noise of an unfamiliar origin. Stepping from the lavatory I peeked into the front room.

There stood Eanin but the voice sounded different even more his actions were altogether diverse. There he was, telling Roo some story of a time in his past making her laugh with every other word. I was happy he pulled through. I had lost faith in mankind before he came along; his previous actions established my reasoning. My inner being desired a lesson was learned.

When the time came to bid all a good night's rest I retired to my room. Shortly after Roo followed displaying a look matching the way I felt. We both agreed on Eanin's behavior being far beyond expectations and altogether respectable. She ended the conversation by reading my mind, "I think you beat some since into that boy."

Sleep had a grip on me; a piercing grip on my chest brought me back abruptly. Her whisper and a finger pointing to a figure's shadow on the curtains sent me to my feet.

Quietly I searched my immediate surrounding for a weapon coming up short. The stranger's silhouette came close, too close to the window. Giving up on the weapon I made my move. The shadow recessed with every step I took. Throwing the curtains back I caught only a glimpse of someone retreating around the corner of the cabin.

Amazing speed took me to the front window only to see an oddly shaped intruder showing me his/her meaning of haste.

Wide-eyed I watched the being flee across the lower field and become lost in the shadows. Roo touched my back softly letting her presents be known but my gaze held to the area I last saw him/her. Quiet and patient she sat while I observed my field of vision.

"Would you wake Lexter? Tell him to come in here, but don't wake Malloy, please." I said softly as possible.

Only seconds passed when she returned only to tell me of a locked door. No matter, the excitement had passed but my uneasiness remained.

Roo stayed close but soon fell asleep. I watched hoping for a return but was relieved there was none. My eyes stayed alert until the sun chased the shadows to their capture. The light gave me comfort, falling asleep before I could tell Lex about the night's occurrence caused disappointment.

For the next few days we were on the lookout. On those nights Lex and I slept in shifts insuring the houses safety. Even on my off time I slept very little if any. My instincts told me the intruder was more than a happenstance. I wanted to believe there was nothing to it, my gut told me otherwise.

Many days fell behind the flow of life. With time came reasons to believe we had nothing to fear. The few crops that generated flourished quickly. The progressing heat indicated summer was within reach. I will admit to my guard being lowered also to there being no justification for why it was.

I was in the lower field with my head down digging in the dirt when his pungent scent warned me of his presents just in time to escape a severe blow to the head.

I quickly scrambled to my feet readying myself to make fight. With sizing my opponent brought a terrifying realization. Not only was I about to clash with the most unnatural individual my eyes had ever seen, I was outnumbered three to one.

Life is full of instances where a person goes against all odds prevailing triumphantly boosting moral for all mankind. This was not one of those instances. My confidence and ability to fight had nothing to do with my outstanding ability in self-preservation.

Remembering the creature's unusual speed kept me from turning my back to run. I had been digging in the dirt with a spade and I believe pointing it at them was the only reason they didn't instantly attack. Deft steps were taken backwards while I examined exactly what I was up against.

The two doing their best to close in on me were two heads shorter than my six feet. If their backs weren't hunched up and if they didn't bow their legs as they swayed left to right they may have been close to my height. Out weighing my 180 lbs. by more than fifty they carried most of it in their shoulders and arms. They handled clubs surprisingly well for having their arms and fingers drawn into S curves.

Bothered by those attributes I was, but their skin and eyes arrested my attention from the rest. Their skin looked painfully fire scorched to the point of being charred and the lifeless color in their eyes seemed hallow. I felt it was of the most importance to keep my eyes fixed on them for the third observed from a short distance atop a black horse.

In a singular glance I obtained a large ominous figure obviously born and bred for one purpose . . . Destroy all whom oppose.

Each step helped me closer to the cabin yet drew the figures inches closer to me. They were in the realm of twelve feet from me and I was nearing one hundred steps from my desired destination when one spoke. "Jussst agree to let usss ssscan you and your blood can ssstay in your body." His voice slithered through the air displaying a snake like demeanor. The other must not have had the ability to speak; he mimicked the other with low hums and grunts smirking all the while.

Doing my best to stall their attack I asked, "Do you think you guys can come back in a couple of days? You know, let me run this over in my brain just to make sure I'm ready." With every few words I was closer.

He paused in thought to my question then quickly dismissed it with a touch of rage. "No now! You mussst anssswer yesss or ansssswer to him." With a crooked finger and a sharp look he indicated the horseman. "What'sss it going to be, tender?"

His voice hissed as the words slid from his tongue making my skin want to crawl off my muscles. The horseman heeled his steed to make up the space I had gained inducing my need to speak.

"If I agree to your demand your boss will scan me and then you will leave?" Closer still.

"Yesss, you and everyone in there."

I was just about where I wanted to be, well within earshot of the cabin. I inhaled deeply to shout as their eyes grew wide anticipating my action.

Before I could release my call for help or either one of my opponents reacted the distinct sound of an arrow cut passed my ear piercing the mute clean through the chest.

The Silver tongued one started to look at his partner causing me to prematurely thrust my spade. Intelligence was not one of his greater qualities, quick reaction and the will to fight was. Blocking my attempt with his club his crooked arm stretched out straight giving him the element of deception. His fingers remained twisted but clenched enough to make a fist that landed on my cheek.

Rolling with the punch I barely evaded his grasp ending up on the ground several feet away. I slid my backhand across my face feeling pain and blood. His skin's texture cut like broken glass and set my blood to a boil as it flowed profusely.

Lexter descended the steps notching an arrow as he came. The horseman came in my direction faster than I anticipated. Lex drew to fire upon Silver tongue sending him in retreat.

Lex must have seen the horseman was dangerously close to me and he redirected his shot. Quick aim followed by an even quicker shot had the horse raring on his hind legs. The arrow deflected off the horses' neck armor sending it into a nearby tree. When the horse came down on all fours I scramble to elude a stomping.

A whip lashed out from the dark rider lassoing my ankle. Speaking aggressively, in a language unknown, he pointed to Lexter and began to drag me behind his horse.

The whip held tight enough to pull me down the hill. Good sense kept me calm and I found my only option. Reaching by means of tenacious strength I pulled off my boot and the whip went with it. I rolled . . .

The rider turned back but my body would not allow escape, Lexter had followed and fired a shot. I turned face to face with the horse, and to see his shot hit its mark.

Before my brother had his last arrow notched the dark rider could not be seen through the wooded path he chose.

My strength was failing and the lights of my world began to grow dim. Lex picked me up, threw me over his shoulder and started towards the cabin. Trauma, drama and blood loss are a bad combination, even worse traveling upside down.

I fought to stay awake to insure everyone I was going to be fine. The last memory I recollect was the sound of Roo screaming my name indistinctly in the distance.

Flashes weaved through the ruins in my mind of soft unfamiliar faces speaking words of encouragement and wisdom. Warmth touched my face inducing pain. I wondered why I could not speak to those speaking to and about me. Only a few times do I remember gaining control of the body I once had known.

My thoughts swam free but confused. Nothing came in any particular order.

I opened my eyes to an unfamiliar room lit by candles with only my body to see. A heavy haze began to lift each passing moment of my consciousness.

Assessing my bodies functions were a priority. I could see and feel the top half of my body, all worked well enough. The bottom half was cover by a blanket.

A slight hesitation drove deep but the need to continue overruled. It took only a few seconds and the bottom complied with every demand.

I hurt to a great extent but the pain could be dealt with since I knew I was not out of order.

A smile radiated a glow brighter than a candle could twice my size. One sigh of relief, one large smile, and a handle turned opening a door to familiar faces regenerating memories clarity.

Chapter IX

Summer had made its way and I did my best to make my way to recovery. Each day my strength grew filling my head with obtainable goals. Most of my pain diminished and that which lingered I began to get use to. The only thing I could not get use to was Eanin's insatiable need to repeatedly apologize for his previous actions. I had not ever been one to hold a grudge . . . forgive and forget? I could not. With subtlety measuring my actions I watched him furtively. The more I watched the more my mind began to change about the boy's demeanor. Was it going to be a lasting effect? One cannot ever know, yet, a change indeed.

Weeks had passed from my awakening and most seemed as if it were the same before our encounter with the creatures. In those weeks we prepared for their return even though there was no promise of such.

After ample restoration, I began to do what I could. I have not ever been able to take much of life simply watching it go by. Taking part by doing ones part should come natural to anyone allowed to breathe. So, as I stated, I did what I could, mainly what my body would allow me to do.

With each passing day more strength returned to my muscles making me quite able to complete necessary tasks. Roo became my sweetened shadow, third hand, most importantly my best friend. Not only did she make me somehow belong in this struggle we called life; her involvement with all situations gave an enjoyable purpose as well.

Lexter and Malloy, now what can I say? They were our rock. Picking up where anyone left off, doing chores from wake to slumber, without a negative comment from either of them.

The most peculiar of all, of course, was Eanin. With every day came a new surprise. There were days he worked a steady pace keeping up with everyone therefore keeping his end of the deal. Moreover were the days he worked his fingers until they bled and a smile all the while as his accomplishments outweighed my own.

Eanin sure made a rough go at first being feisty, well flat out poisonous. The way he had shaped up, screwed his head on tight, and dug his heals in made me think he had learned a valuable lesson.

The youth need stern guidance but overall they need to be needed, trusted, and someone who will listen for understanding them. Most of the time when given those things the young will come around sooner than later and if not; a good old fashion butt kicking will do it.

One late evening the night air regenerated memories of times previous to our problematic situation. Thinking of both I mentioned not one negative word as we all conversed under a sky filled with stars. The wind was stirred the smoke in a cyclone lifting it beyond our senses. We did not have much but each other, a small fire and the moment. The serenity presented was cherished beyond comprehension.

Our dwindling fire burned, not for warmth, for it was just enjoyable to have. Lex spoke of times when he and I were young, spending summers with our family in that very cabin. My breath eluded my grasp from time to time seeing the fire light dance on Roo's seemingly perfect features. When she stole glances at me I felt a blast of electricity incapacitating my body and I began to melt inwardly.

Conversation took a hard turn when Lexter had mentioned a comical threat my father, Neol, gave every time Lex or I were insolent, "If you boys don't quit your fussing I'm gonna take ya behind the wood shed and whip ya good." It instilled an idea, which would not only give a protected retreat in case we were attacked again also provide a sense of self-preservation.

Eanin was the first to fall asleep under monotone voiced stories, a sky filled with stars and firelight. Seeing him do so gave us all a sense of security inducing everyone but myself to follow suit.

Morning came as quick as the rain lifting us all to our feet in a race for shelter. Entering the cabin with great gasps of breath we all gazed each other over. We were a pitiful sight, still shaking dreams from our hair along with the rain and soaked clear through to the bone. Our gaze only last a short moment before we burst out into hysterical laughter. The euphoria was quickly snuffed out by a thunderous crash of struck lightning.

The lightning caught us off guard but the next event took us from our feet. Violently the ground began to shake with a force and we fell to the floor. The girls screamed at the height of their ability presenting a chill that ran the length of my spine.

All was silent. Calmness and serenity methodically restored itself to our surroundings.

The annals of the morning left us speechless. Wonder and apprehension sculpted our faces as they were. How the old cabin held itself together through the violence of which we had just endured I will not ever know. Thinking such made me even more elated of my family's ability to construct.

The rain lingered for several hours yielding not much more than a plan of action for the escape route we were to build. About the moment my lackadaisical attitude took full grasp of my will to resist, the rain stopped.

We hesitated none at all. We raced into action with elbows and footfalls. By the time the last ray of light dissipated our secrete passage was crude, yet, complete. With that water under the bridge I slept a bit more sound.

We had rationed our usage of provisions quite well. Yet, no matter how well one manages a source, in time it will diminish.

There we were scant provisions and not a one of us wanting to return to Hector for more . . . besides Eanin.

It did not take long before Lex and I gave in to Eanin's insistent, moreover, insatiable need to prove his self-worth. After all he bore the mark and what was left on his account after his first purchase in Hector would be more than sufficient of our needs.

I had only just started my briefing on the importance of his trip to and from town before Roo sharply reverted my thinking by cutting me off.

"I have to go with him to check on Uncle Charles!"

Giving my all to talk calmly I stated, "I think it would be best if Eanin traveled alone."

Biting her pursed lip and turning red by the breath she held, nothing more was said as she retreated to the bedroom.

"Eanin, you best be . . ."

Cut off once again by Roo's displaced aggression presented by a slamming door causing me to bite my lip as well.

Eyes wide with questionable anxiety fell on me by each person in the room. This was a first time occurrence. I had, like most people in a new relationship, hoped an argument would not happen.

Lex took the floor and I searched for wisdom as I walked towards the bedroom door.

Paralysis enveloped me while reaching for the door's knob. I did not want to hurt Roo's feelings any more than I wanted to tell her what to do. Though, I made a deal with her Uncle Charles and I meant to keep it. With such in mind entering through the door came with no greater ease.

There she was, lumped up in a ball in the middle of the bed, sobbing to beat the band. Now, I have not ever been a connoisseur of emotion but have found just being there for someone can prove a great deal.

Sitting down within reach I inhaled her aroma deeply. When I laid my hand upon her shoulder she did not move. Neither did I. Feeling her precious little body shuddering with every breath nearly caused me to speak. Yet, I kept to my motto; a wise man speaks when he has something to say, a fool will speak because he thinks he has to. With my tongue between my teeth I did my best to stay wise.

Within a short time her pattern of breath became regular and calmness restored as she peaked out through her arm-crossed self-imprisonment.

Spoken, as softly as passed beyond the lips of some mystical angel she said simply, "I understand."

With her words came her embrace and after came a light kiss from my lips landing on a teardrop that drown the situation.

Eanin was ready for the word go but we needed the full day to access all necessary provisions and filter all wants aside. With a few words he complied. Surprisingly enough he threw in a good idea of supplies we sorely needed and may have forgotten if he had not mentioned.

It was a most uncomfortable night as I tossed and turned while crossing imaginary bridges on Eanin's mission road. I was not at all feeling confident with our conclusive decision. No other choice had been presented leaving out even the possibility of a process of elimination.

Roo was bothered none at all for she slept as sound as her beauty was radiant.

I was on the brink of admitting failure to crossing sleep's threshold when without warning I fell.

Ominously my dreams crept through the catacombs of my mind. Pieces of my life's puzzle fell away into a vast void, leaving me unimaginably nonexistent. Within endless space, further than my mind's eye could comprehensively see was not a light but a purpose. This purpose had no particular shape yet, somehow I knew it existed. Beyond reach I stood, motionless trying to call it near with a silent voice.

A flash of consciousness merited an ending to my disturbing dream. A still framed image of Roo's sweet essence enveloped in sleep, accentuated by slightly lighted surroundings, gave purchase to my return to slumber.

The next moment I involuntarily joined the living, I was alone

For briefly a moment I lay so still, taking in the senses of life. Not a conjectural thought arrested my mind other than the simplest notice of existence.

Alone? I had slept late, usually unusual for me. Roo, in normality, slept much later than I, this thought alone made my nature quite inquisitional. Arising from my bed a search for occupants was conducted.

The morning had done its best to evade my awareness by nearly passing the hour of noon. Calling a few times with no answer in return I stepped out only to find my shadow doing its best to evade me as well.

Noon it was. Not a soul in sight. A thin bead of sweat began to form on my forehead; the wicked smell of fear pierced my nostril, a sickening pain grew rapidly within my chest.

Alone! Pressure . . . this cannot be! Inhaling deeply to release a scream in hopes of reaching every crevasse within those broken hills I froze. Laughter from a distance held my tongue.

It was nearly impossible to transfix my hearing on the laughter's exact origin for the wind was in a forceful mood. I waited, listening, hoping for the sound to make its way to me again. Was it real? Or was it evil laughing with the knowledge of my desertion.

The laughter had turned to an indistinct tone of mild conversation and no doubt coming from within the cabin. Wondering why my calls were not answered I returned inside.

Lex and Malloy were ascending from the depths of the cellar. My patience was at the end of its length in not knowing Roo's whereabouts. They had reached the height of the cabin. Before one solitary syllable reached the tip of their tongue in question or statement I fired from the lip. "Where are Roo and Eanin?"

Malloy winced as if the reverb of my voice had power enough to move her. Lex grimacing slightly answered, "Didn't know if you were ever going to wake up little bro so, I told Eanin it was alright for him to get on with it. I didn't want him to be out so long that he had to return in the dark." Clearing his throat as Malloy quietly stepped around him to carry on with her duties he continued, "Roo? Hasn't she been in there sleeping with you?"

Fire from within my chest splayed throughout every vein contained inside my body. The intensity of the flame was so evident Lex took a step backwards surely in fear of being scorched. His mouth opened, not to speak, to let out an empathetic breath of exasperation.

Turning on my heel in direction of my room I made my way quickly. Before I could reach the doorway Lex changed my motive with a single word, which may have been the only one to help me change my action. "Think!"

In doing so I quickly realized I could not follow into the shadows of which she had chosen to travel. I could only hope of her safe return.

For a time unknown I remained motionless, as if I were paralyzed from within. Over, over, again and again I turned the predicament through my twisting mind. So many times I had warned myself, yet I did not listen? No!

Scarcely do we take our own advice especially when it comes to the act of opening our hearts to the thought of love then only to have it beaten, thrown to and fro. Oh, so violently that somewhere between the volley and destination it dissipates from refraction.

She had made me believe all was well to calm my thoughts, yet, with a motive as selfish as a serpent.

Thoughts such as these then multiplied to an astronomical proportion squeezed every ounce of energy within my being. I did my best to displace my torturous mind with a feeble act of bussing myself. Every object touched I wanted to break. Everywhere looked, I saw only red. With stench in my nostrils and a furrowed brow I bathed in the fuel of hate.

Moments lapsed. My malicious thoughts subside. As the day lingered on, calmness regained. Shadows elongated and sanity returned only a few short breaths before the vehicle containing my little runaway returned.

The vehicle approached discerningly until they noticed I waited upon the porch. The vehicle slowed, by the time I could clearly see their frightened featured faces the vehicle crept forward barely noticeable.

Eanin was the first of the two to make a move. He had reached the bottom of the step as Roo opened her door. I could tell he was expecting me to burst out in some catastrophic act of malicious violence towards him. It was not within me to displace my aggression.

"Rison, man please don't be mad! She told me you two worked it out and that it was fine if she went. When we pulled in the drive, right back there," pointing at the entrance to the field he continued, "she told me the truth."

As he gazed under his brow he began to plead, "I swear man, I had no idea. I . . ."

Cut off by my raised hand I proceeded to assure him he was not at fault and to continue with the task of bringing supplies into the house. With quickness he returned to the vehicle complying with my request.

Roo was gathering a few sacks from the rear of the vehicle when I approached. A gasp escaped her as she looked into my piercing eyes. She started to speak, ultimately coming up shorter than a single word. I followed suite for I had no words as well.

Eanin was close to the door of the cabin when the thought arose and the question sprang, "Did you keep a close watch on your back trail?" The look on his face answered the question immediately.

Omniscient of Eanin's feelings for Roo and just how distracting her beauty can be I shook my head with understanding as he made entrance to the cabin.

Roo started for the cabin, I had only one question to ask, "How is your Uncle Charles?"

Turning towards me, yet, not looking directly at me she answered in a low, pitiful voice, "He wasn't even there. The lady running the store said he hadn't been there for several days."

Sarcasm played a tune for I spoke before thinking, "Then the trip was well worth the damage caused."

With a quick evil glare followed by an even quicker retreat into the cabin I was again left to my lonesome. Not to say I minded it so much at the time.

Two sacks of supplies remained. Taking them within my grasp I started for the cabin only to be frozen by a low rumble in the distance. Crouching by the side of the vehicle I watched in the direction of the noise.

Oh, I thought, it could not be. They led them right to us. A light gleamed through the tree line. I was sure it was another vehicle making its way.

Moments passed. Into full view they came. There was a motorcade of three. I dropped the sacks and made for the cabin to warn the others. Just before I ascended the steps the vehicle in front gave a slight honk.

I received from the sound a positive as opposed to a negative feeling. So, I waited as the space between us diminished.

I could tell there were at least twelve occupants in the procession, though, were quite unsure. Not a one looked familiar. Until the back door on the first vehicle swung open on its hinges revealing Charles.

Fully expecting him to have a smile on his face but just the opposite completely changed my relief into concern.

Charles was looking in the direction of the two sacks sitting at the back of our vehicle. Knowing I was going to get a word or three about letting Eanin go into town I could do nothing to stop them from coming.

"Have ya lost your mind boy? I thought I told ya not to go back into town."

"He didn't, Eanin and I did." Roo said from the cabin.

When I turned back to Charles I was ready for a cussing. Not for what he did.

Spun into a half circle by a right jab I had to take a moment to realize what just happened. I started to throttle the old man before I thought it through and before I reached him Roo screamed my name fully stopping me.

I guess I deserved what he gave. I was trusted with his niece and to him, it surely seemed, I was not keeping my end of the bargain.

By the time Roo explained the situation all the passengers had exited the vehicles and were looking around, stretching, taking in the serenity. My count was unnoticed yet coming up with the number fourteen.

I wasn't sure the old cabin could accommodate such a number but kept that to myself.

Stars began to show themselves and the weight of the day I began to feel. With a few words of suggestion we all retreated to the cabin in hopes of finding a piece of comfort and suitable sleeping arrangements.

Chapter X

The smell in the air was one so strange. Right out of one's touch making it nearly impossible to put a finger on and lacking elements seeming to suffocate. I was quite uncomfortable. Seeing the cabin crowded with the newly acquired occupants caused wonder to the future and gave question to the past.

For the most part each of the fourteen was of good health, aged in their prime and without a doubt unmarked. After Charles attended to their sleeping arrangements he pulled Lex and me outside.

He asked us to help him retrieve a few items out of the rear of one of the vehicles. We gave no question and he had said no more.

Charles opened the hatch revealing the items and what was seen gave proof to the statement he had made several months before, "Hope y'all are ready for war." Even after we had been warned and at that point standing in front of a massive amount of weapons I was as ready as I was when this had begun, none at all.

In a tone barely auditable Charles advised to pick out a weapon best suitable for us but directing with his opinion. "Logan, ya should take one of 'em there bows, a good heap of arrows, and double edged dagger."

Lexter gathered his supplies as Charles handed me one of the oldest of his acquired fighting weapons. A two-edged sword nearly three feet long and by the feel of it weighed close to three pounds. It felt good; it had been a long time.

Once again Charles had proven his relationship with our father ran as deep as any river known and the words that followed stifled any wonder. "Now we'll see if 'em lessons 'at pa of yours gave you boys is gonna pay off."

As my brother and I grew up our father taught us quite a bit on just about every weapon imaginable. As we became young men he had honed in on the weapons we had felt most comfortable with causing us to excel in a weapon of choice.

With one glace at by brother the look on his face gave understanding we were thinking the exact same thing. All those hours practicing with our father had much more of a purpose than just keeping us occupied. He was readying us for a fate he knew would come. With the help of one of father's close friends we were aware the time was upon us.

Roo had come out of the cabin driven by concern and asked the nature of our disappearance. Charles assured her all was well and asked her to return for we would be in soon.

"You boys sleep with those weapons almighty close to ya at all times. War is come'n and come'n quick." After those words left his mouth he started for the cabin and we let him go.

When my thoughts had slowed themselves enough to allow sleep I was by my lonesome. Dreams came and went barely noticed. I woke but I did not wake alone. I had my blade and in that moment it was all I needed for I woke to the sound of battle. The thunderous crash of metal on metal and screams originating from the depths of one's soul set me into fast action.

Blade unsheathed I hurled through an empty cabin with sweat on my brow and fire flowing within my veins. Bursting beyond the cabin into the open my heart raced, anxiety gripped every nerve, and I was ready for war . . . or so I thought.

"Practicing!" All inhabitance of the cabin were merely practicing! At the moment my feelings were so uncertain I did not know how to react. Before a decision was made Lexter made my presents well known with a comment turning all heads in my immediate direction, "Glad to have you join us little brother, yet, I do not believe we all share your enthusiasm."

Laughter began to echo throughout the broken hills. Momentarily confused I was, until clarity enveloped me of their reason for making fun. It takes two attributes of one's exterior to make ready for battle, a weapon and armor . . . or at the very least clothing.

I could only be upset with myself for being made such a spectacle. What else to do but join in on the fun and laugh as well?

"Get yourself some clothes and a cup of java then join us. We need to get some practice." Lex stated as he was doing his best not to look directly at me for fear of another outburst.

No sooner did the suggestion come before action was made.

It did not take much time at all to regain my ability with use of the sword. Moments passed when it was close to unnoticeable that I had been several years without a blade in my hand. Also, I did not know the newcomers well but after a few days of practicing hand to hand combat one will grow to know his companions quite rapidly. One of my favorites was a man named Jonas. He handled the sword well and was an enormous brute of a man. I was glad to on his side.

I was elated to find my relationship with the sword was sound, but I was quite discontent with the rapid dissipation of my relationship with Roo. She was elusive in those days. I can't say I blame her for I was not in a convivial mood.

The sun's rise on the fourth day brought awareness, the sound of battle caused clarity but the smell of smoke changed my thoughts entirely. Exiting my room, fully clothed,

I found the cabin inflamed completely. I yelled to the extent of my ability receiving no answer. There was no way through or around the fire. My lungs felt heavy and my eyes burned dreadfully. My only option was the crude escape route. I took it with no further hesitation.

Heat blasted my backside while exiting the cabin. Only hope remained in those moments for I had absolutely no idea if I were the only survivor of our group. Either way, I was to face the fate, which laid ahead, no matter if it meant my demise.

The passageway we had made was dark; the ceiling was low and led to the shed. I moved slowly seeing light ahead knowing I was close to the end of the passage wondering what else may be there waiting for me.

The smell of death was in the air and I liked it none at all. My heart raced but my hand was as calm as stone as it gripped my sword. Reaching the end of the passage I noticed tracks left by ones whom used the same route of escape. I began to study them briefly and the noise of gravel being compressed by timid footsteps readied me for my oncoming opponent. A shadow formed at the corner not four feet away from me. It was time . . .

Softly filling my ears was a familiar whisper, "Rison?" It was Lexter.

Still alive! The image of my brother brought hope. Between that very moment and the end of our journey there was an exuberant amount of possibilities but in that instant hope was revived.

"Lex, good to see your face brother even if it does have blood all over it." I said with concern.

"Don't you worry little brother it's not my blood. It seems the creatures we encountered a while ago came back tenfold teaming up with the B.E.A.S.T." He informed as we both searched our surroundings for enemies.

"Where are the girls?" I ask as I gripped my sword a bit tighter.

"I sent them to the cave. You remember the cave don't you?"

The cave resided nearly two hundred yard behind the cabin down a thickly timbered hill, over a spring fed stream and on the face of rock wall. A place visited periodically by Lex and me when we were children. Thinking such I simply answered, "Yes."

"We need to get to them and start moving, we have to get as far away from this place a possible and I mean now!"

I had not a word to add and with a solitary glace Lex was fully assured with my readiness by the expression on my face.

We had covered nearly half the distance to the stream when a strange and loathsome aroma loaded the air filling my nostrils ultimately heightening my senses to an unfathomable degree. Slowing our pace we noticed several creatures separated us from the stream. They stood about studying the ground, no doubt, doing their best to decipher the location of the girls.

I felt the touch of my brother's hand on my shoulder breaking me free from the bridges I was crossing in my mind. He spoke only loud enough for me to hear, "Not one of those creatures shall live."

Leaves and branches lightly scraped our clothing as we stealthy, moreover, savagely pursued in the direction of the enemy. The space between the inevitable confrontation closed rapidly and an accurate number of our opponents were calculated. There were six bodies, to be seen, standing as if terrified to cross the stream. Five of the six were like the creatures we had encountered once before and one resembled the characters in black we had evaded in the city.

The man in black insisted, with loud voice and bodily gestures, the creatures subdue to his command by crossing the stream, with no avail.

Mesmerized by their leader and enthralled by his leadership our presence was undetected giving us an element, of much needed, surprise. We came from the woods with ferocity, force, and with only one objective, to annihilate.

Lexter had let fly an arrow, taking down the leader, and hit his second mark just as I had taken my first head. With knowledge of my brother's inner workings if I didn't make quick labor, to even the number, he would not likely let me live it down.

The creatures scattered slightly by our initial attack but regrouped swiftly with their battle faces on. With hatred in my eyes and ice flowing throughout my veins I advanced on my next victim, him having a sword as well.

My second intention put him en garde in the exact opposite direction I intended to lunge as I slid my blade down the side of his neck cutting it half through. Remising on the third, in my attack, I felt an astute pain shifting my equilibrium sending me headlong into the stream. My last vision was that of Eanin (from a distance), falling to the ground with an arrow protruding from his throat.

Dark waves lapped over my throbbing skull. The smell of fresh spring water and carnage filled my soul. Towering above me was a warrior atop a fiery red horse shouting orders, in an unknown tongue, pointing a finger in my definite direction. Moments previous I was sure death had consumed me yet, I rose from the place that should have been my grave. It was not by my own strength did I rise, but by the assistance of the creatures for I felt their skin's distinct abrasiveness clasp my arms pulling me erect.

My consciousness came and went in minute spurts only allowing me the realization of being partially amongst the living. I knew not of where the B.E.A.S.T. was taking me but embedded deep within my mind I knew my existence was going to be perpetually altered.

A wretched sickness enveloped me during my next momentary surge of awareness. I was in a place I had only read about but had hoped I would not ever witness, a penitentiary. I tried with my remaining strength to break free from my captures only to find my strength fail me miserably. The voices echoed, I could not understand but one single phrase, "Take this one to chamber eight."

For a while I don't remember much. Only bits and pieces of my past flashed constant reminders of hope I once sustained.

Chapter XI

Slowly my awareness had presented itself and I was utterly alone. No light to be had, no sound but the ringing in my ears could be heard, and my head swam ever so slightly. Hunger ailed just before deep inhaling stench from the years of neglect my surroundings had attained turned my stomach. Crawling on hands and knees I began my search.

Below me was damp concrete dusted with particles of miscellaneous debris no larger than specks of dirt. I shuffled forward awkwardly, with one hand stretched out, desperately probing for anything to fill my grasp. I had only moved a few feet before I thrust my hand out viciously, finding what I sought but in return bending my fingernail off its rightful placement. With that I groaned intensely.

After pushing my nail back, as best I could, I reached again but much more adeptly. There was a wall just as hard, damp, and dirty as the floor I was upon. Holding my hand flat against the wall for assurance and stability I elevated myself to full height.

To an uncountable degree of time I scouted the cage of my imprisonment, counting my steps, calculating the spaces between objects, coming up with a suitable image in my mind of the surroundings.

The chamber was eight feet wide by the same amount of space long. The height of the ceiling was only two and a half feet above my head. I had a concrete protrusion from the wall standing nearly two feet high, three feet wide, and about six feet long. There was a sink and toilet, which felt like it was all connected together into one unit. Neither had running water but the toilet did have some sort of flap that opened and closed directly into a pipeline. I could feel the door and what, at some time far past by, could have been a window of sort.

Completely exhausted I extended myself out onto the protrusion with hunger and thirst as my companions. Thoughts of my brother and the others nearly consumed my sanity before alerted by the sound of an unlocking door.

My eyes were so accustomed to the darkness that when the door opened I could scarcely see what had happened. Hearing the sound of materials hitting the floor I cautiously made my way in its direction.

In the floor lay a pile of substance resembling my captures version of food. I couldn't stand the smell of what was before me and it was beyond my realm of thinking to consume it off the filth, which it resided.

Returning to my bed of concrete I invoked misery and harbored hate. I did not know how or when I was going to escape from this state of penitence; by mustering every fiber of my woven inner being it would be done.

Days, maybe even weeks passed uncalculated, unnoted for time stood still, I began to wither away in hunger. The rotted food on the floor was no more, for the insects and rats had taken it from me. My strength was near none when once again the key entered, lock recessed, and a pile of rubbish landed on the floor. Instantly I landed before it, face down, shoveling handfuls in my mouth doing my best to choke it down. I could no longer taste. My senses dulled to mere existence and existence alone I merely felt. Twice I had to slap a rodent away from my pile of food and both times I was bitten badly. I had lost all pride. The man, I had once known myself to be, was no more.

When I had all I could take, of the so-called food, I started to worm my way back to my resting place when the door sadistically swung open. Two men swarmed me swiftly covering my head with a gunnysack and proceeded to drag me out of my chamber. I had no strength to make fight, I could only let them do whatever it was they were to do.

By sight it was near impossible to distinguish anything beyond the sack. It did not occur to me, until I was well on my way, due the manner in which I had been taken, to count the footfalls of my detainees. I did surmise an approximate count, added to directions taken, plus obstacles involved. Nearly thirty steps led to a sharp left turn, close to the same amount of steps we halted for a door to be opened. Once through the door they drug me what felt like just a few feet before we turned half circle then descending a flight of stairs. I did my best to count the number of times the top of my feet fell making contact with the adjacent descending step but by the end of the flight my number had lost itself amongst my confusion.

The light shown through the sack was dim; the air was stale and damp as if we were in a storm cellar rarely used.

I was hoisted to some sort of table where my arms and legs were fastened securely. Instantaneous to the final synching the sack was removed revealing a silhouetted character that began working my head into an apparatus. The device was made of thick leather straps enveloping my head resembling a helmet.

I could only see what was directly in front of my face and I saw it coming. Four metal prongs held together by brackets, and a threaded shaft resembling some sort of vice intended to be inserted into my mouth for prying it open. I wanted no part of it so I bit a finger of the administer meriting a slug in the throat giving him the right of passage for insertion.

A familiar voice materialized from the darkness of my surroundings, "You ssshould have let usss ssscan you long ago tender. Would have sssave you sssome pain."

My eyes were closed for only a moment previous to those words and feeling an excruciating pinch on my nose allowed me to only breathe out of my mouth, my eyes were wide with hate focusing on Silver Tongue.

"At anytime you want me to ssstop giving you what you dessserve to take the mark, all you have to do isss tell me, then I will ssstop, you'll be marked, then releasssed." He said as he slightly swayed hovering above me holding a flagon of liquid over my mouth letting a portion of the fluid fill my throat causing me to choke violently.

He waited a moment, allowing me to gain composure, hoping for a response he desperately wanted to hear. Instead I did my best to formulate the words, "You shall not have me."

The liquid came in a steady flow. No reprieve was given and no sympathy allowed for my torture was well warranted through the eyes of my torturer.

In those moments of terror I had feelings more intense than I have ever encountered before. Anxiety, concentrated suffocation, or even the simplest fact of longing for the shadow of death to take me can compare none at all to the state I was in.

My life hung in the balance between a terrible state of existence and a death not willing to have me. The only option was to endure this plague upon me for I had no other choice.

For a moment I was sure the liquid had stopped flowing, just as sure that I could not taste the foul air around me. Their haunting laughter was still ringing in my ears when pressure was applied causing me to expel the fluid from my lungs meriting a continuance of the torture.

I have no clue as to how long I endured the drowning table, it was seemingly endless. My next recollection was finding myself on the floor in my chamber.

Desolate and dark emotions filled my thoughts as did it shroud my surroundings. My throat was raw and my abdomen hurt so horrific I could hardly breathe. I became insufferably ill. With my remaining strength I drug myself to the stainless steel toilet reaching it just in time to vomit aggressively. I did so far beyond the point of having anything left within me besides bile and blood.

A blanket of depression lay upon me. The fire I had burning deep within my being was near to snuffed out leaving my soul dim and without substance.

Oh, how the mind will reach out for comfort when there is none to be had. I searched for a single shred of hope coming up sort. My body would not comply with any demand I presented, yet, my mind raced even though I pleaded it not to.

The simple presence of company we enjoy, the taste of pleasantries on our tongue, a clean article of clothing resting upon our skin, the sound of wind dancing through a nearby forest, the sight of birds playing chase in the sky, reading a book by firelight to a loved one, or rain cleansing our spirit as it plummets from freedom's sky has less meaning until it is no more.

We as humans seem to see best in retrospect. If hindsight were foresight life would take on a completely different meaning.

In despair and solitude came a sound through the pipeline of which I had been vomiting. It was the voice of a man ensuring me that he could help. Was I dreaming, or . . .

Some time had passed with no visits from my captures. Then they came, the demeanor of their coming confused me heavily. They brought with them food, real food, and clean water for drinking. Though my taste buds were in a sort of remission I enjoyed every morsel keeping silence to the fact.

It took me but an instant to realize the purpose of their fastidious behavior. They were bringing me back to health to torture me further.

Still not knowing if my encounter with the man in the pipeline was fantasy or reality I believed it to be the latter. Periodically I pushed the flap open speaking with anticipation but receiving no response. Tenacious effort despite my minds doubts brought a reply reviving moral to a heighten state beyond comprehension.

His name was Loren. He too was held captive against his will and informed me of our location, Strington. It was a prison well known to the vicinity of my upbringing far away from any inhabitants.

The guards checked on me occasionally but when they did I pretended to worse off than I was eager do delay inevitability. Conversations between Loren and I did not ever last long but it was pleasurable all the same. Many different subjects we touched upon, the most important was the way he was to pass me a particular item.

Strength within my being was well regenerated and sleep was well underway when I heard the door's hinges creak, my movement was quick but not quick enough.

The same route was taken as before. Knowing what I went through before sickened me to an uncontrollable vomiting reaction when reaching the descending stairs.

Entrance to the lower level of the compound was made and awaiting our arrival was the Silver-tongued creature. Beside him was a chair. Into the chair I was placed, bound to the arms and legs securely. One of the two that brought me retrieved a mechanism from a nearby table. The tool was a shaft, threaded for adjustments with flat prongs on both ends. It also came equipped with a circular strap resembling a belt and buckle.

The shaft was placed in the divot below my neck located between my collarbones; extending under my chin, adjusted to such a degree my jaw was sealed shut, and belted around my neck. After all was in place one of my captures took out a knife and assured me if I looked away from what was happening they would cut my eyelids open.

Across the room was a device of sheer terror I had read about when I was a boy. They called it the Spanish Donkey. It was a solid block of wood cut into a triangle standing nearly six feet tall with the most extreme point directed upward. On either side of the device were weights connected to short leather straps.

There was a rustling from the top of the stairs and the distinct sound of another prisoner being drug down the stairs. This prisoner must have known what awaited him for he screamed with all that was within him as he came.

They took him before the device and the Silver tongued creature stooped before me staring me directly into my unblinking eyes stating, "If you don't let usss ssscan you tender your fate will be the sssame asss thisss one."

Then the man was stripped of his clothing, fastened to a hoist, and elevated astride the triangle block. The man's face had entered the light and was familiar, yes I knew him.

It felt as if a lifetime had passed since I had seen a recognizable face. His name was Jonas. One of the fourteen people Charles had brought to the cabin. He was the large character that Jonas, strong willed, and good with a sword. I remembered practicing with him well. The day battle broke out at the cabin I am quite certain he brought many to their demise and did not come quietly.

His health looked well bringing accuracy to my thoughts on being brought near to full strength for further torture.

There he was, astride the triangle block looking at me directly. I wanted to help him but I could not, I could only watch.

Two guards worked in one motion readying the weights for placement. Silver tongue left my side to give Jonas his last opportunity, "Comfortable tender? When those bagsss are placssed on your anklesss you're really going to enjoy yoursssself. Thisss iss the lassst time I'm going to asssk, will you take the mark?

Jonas' remark was barely auditable. Silver tongue took a few crooked steps forward landing him only a short distance away demanding Jonas to; "SSSpeak up!"

Blood and saliva ejected from Jonas' mouth hitting his mark, directly into the eyes of Silver tongue.

Fueled by hate and embarrassment Silver tongue screamed, "SSStrap them on!"

I wanted to look away—I could not. I wanted to stop his pain—I could not. I wanted to cover my ears to impede the sound of a man being ripped in half—I could not. Just when I started to feel faint the ground began to shake.

I was jolted from my upright position by an earthquake landing on my side still strapped to the chair.

Particles from the walls and ceiling began to vibrate free landing themselves on the surrounding floor. The lights had gone out leaving all silent, which for a fleeting moment was pleasant, until I realized I did not hear Jonas' screams anymore. The lights regenerated revealing him split into two pieces piled lifeless upon the floor.

I struggled to break free from my chair but I was bound tight. Before I had much of a chance to think the guards were standing my chair erect and Silver tongue was about my face point his crooked finger in Jonas' direction informing me, "If you don't take the mark tender that'sss what'sss going to happen to you."

He let the thought resonate before he demanded me back to my chamber. As the guards were dragging me away I could hear Silver tongue say, "Three moonsss tender, have your ansssswer in three moonsss."

Chapter XII

In dismay and silence I contemplated my situation. Would I ever see the light of day outside the prison's walls, hear the soothing effects of a women's voice, or feel freedom's breath upon my face? Was I to die as Jonas had? Was this the end?

The stain of Jonas being torn apart embedded itself into my mind's eye tormenting my thoughts leaving me in a state of paralysis. A whistling sound pulled me back to reality. Quickly I was on my hands and knees in search of the source. It was coming from the corner of my chamber partially hidden by the concrete protrusion and toilet.

Lightening struck revealing a series of cracks admitting sight to the outside world. The earthquake had given me chance and that chance I would take.

I began to claw, push, and pry at each block with inhuman like force to no avail, save one. I was so excited I did not realize how loud I was until the distinct sound of voices originated outside my chamber's door. Quickly I replaced the block and threw myself over the stainless steel toilet, began slapping its side, and giving my best performance of imitating a sickly vomiting state.

The door was opened followed by the sound of laughter from a pair of guards. "You should just take the mark you fool and we will let you go." One of the guards mentioned as the other carried on with his laughter then they slammed the door shut. For a moment I just sat there breathing heavily hoping they would not return.

Pushing the flap open I called into the pipeline. Loren answered with instructions on how I was to receive an item he was sending.

The prison was a multi level building with each chamber directly above another allowing each toilet to empty into the same pipeline and the only trap existing below the lowest level permitting a straight shot from one to the next.

"I hope your hands are not too large to fit through the hole in your toilet my friend or this is not going to work." Loren said sounding a little uneasy. "If you can get your hand inside feel for a cord and once you get hold of the cord give me a little tug so I know you're ready."

My mother had told me when I was young that I would have made a great pianist for my hands were long and slender. Fortunately that attribute had stayed with me.

Touching my thumb to my pinky finger and pyramiding the other three my hand slid through the hole with a maneuvering push. Instantaneously I felt the thin cord but it took a moment for me to get it and my hand back through the hole. Once I did I gave a tug and I heard something coursing its way through the pipeline ultimately giving a jerk when it ran out of cord. With haste as my guide and apparition as my fuel I pulled the object from within. It was a piece of metal about eight inches long and honed to a point on one end. Also tied to the cord was a piece of parchment. It was too dark to tell what was on the parchment but I knew if were important enough to risk sending it to me it was important enough to hold on to.

I spoke into the pipeline to thank Loren for the items and to ask what was on the parchment but received no answer. I heard screaming outside my chamber door. Swiftly I moved to the door placing my ear against it only to hear Loren's voice retreating beyond reach.

Loren was either going to be tortured or killed this I was sure. Not to be unsympathetic of his situation but if the guards were busy with him they were less likely going to pay me much attention. So to work on the wall I went.

Desperately I removed the first block receiving a fresh breath of air filling my inner being giving me energy I had long been without. Rain blasted my arm as I extended through the opening. Cupping my hand I gathered small portions of rain bring them back, gingerly, to my parched lips. I drank all I could careful not to disturb the dirt upon my face for fear the guards would notice. Thinking such I took dirt from the floor rubbing it on my hand and up my arm.

Several hours later I had removed three blocks, resembling an L shape, then placed them back to await the right timing. In a few hours food would be brought and I needed rest if my escape was to be successful.

Returning to my concrete bed I tossed and turned eventually falling from consciousness. Hours had passed in slumber and I awoke long before the food came giving me a chance to block all possible light from entering through the cracks using dirt off the floor.

Night was in full force and soon I was to make my move. I had food in my stomach and was working on more sleep. The pitch of night would be my companion as I made my way to freedom's shore.

All was going according to plan and I was sure nothing could stand in my way. Opening my eyes I saw light and heard the slithering voice of Silver tongue asking out loud, "What'sss thisss?" He was alone, staring into the corner of my camber.

In a single motion I was on my feet. He had redirected his flashlight on me and started to yell for assistance. Before he could utter a word I slipped the piece of honed metal from my waistband and thrust it deep into his throat.

He hit the floor clawing at his neck only aggravating his condition. I had no opportunity to think, the time was upon me to react and react I did.

I pulled the blocks away from their placement and lay on my front side sliding my feet first out through the opening. Grasping onto the edge I fought frantically for a foothold and found none. I had no idea how far away the ground was and I did not want to let go.

Lightning flashed giving me exactly what I needed. The drop would only be about ten or twelve feet, I pushed myself off the wall and fell.

I landed on my feet momentarily; the ground was saturated with the passing rain and as soon as my feet touched they slid out from under me landing me on my back. Immediately I was running with all my might looking behind as much as in front.

In one of the instances that I was looking behind I came head on with a fence knocking me down. Before I even realized I was down I was scaling the fence. When reaching the top I was cut by razor wire. I ripped my shirt off and wrapped it around one of my hands guiding the wire to one side, stepped up, and threw myself over. On my descent I felt the wire catch my arm slicing me open from the elbow to fingertip. As I kept moving I rewrapped my shirt around my mangled arm hoping it would slow the bleeding. It was dark, my heart raced with intensity, I was soaked with blood and sweat but for the moment I was free.

Tentative assumptions riddled my empirical consequences every step I made further away from that prison. Delirium caused my pace to slow but the thought of returning kept me moving on.

Periodically lightning flashed in the distance giving me direction. Many times I fell and just that many times I rose. If I wanted keep my freedom I had to put as much space between myself and the prison as I possibly could.

The sky began to show evidence of a coming morning and fog lay heavy around my waist. In the remote distance I spotted a sycamore tree signifying there was a stream or river nearby. Briefly I was upon it and a river it was.

Just before I started to cross the thought of parchment entered my mind. Taking it from my pocket I opened the folds revealing a map indicating my location.

The prison was clearly marked and the river was there as well. What looked like a circle with an x stricken through it was adjacent to the river downstream. There was something written at the bottom of the page but it was not quite light enough for me to decipher what it read. In the immediate direction of the x I fled.

When the sun made its way over the horizon I read what Jonas had written.—My home, take what you need-

My eyes stayed alert to my surroundings as I made my way downstream. Paranoia accompanied my lonely journey along the river's side. The breeze stirred slightly bringing with it the sound of howling dogs.

It had to be my captures searching for me.

Franticly I moved faster and a small shack came into view. It was across the river and I dove in headfirst. There was no choice but remove my boots upon entering the water. If I were to evade my captures and not drown in the process I had to let them go. Once I did my swimming ability progressed rapidly. Hand over hand breath after breath I fought the current achieving my goal.

Seeing a dock protruding from the river's bank I made my way to it. Just as I clasp my arms around one of the polls a fierce cramp took control of my left leg. Biting my lip I did best to make not a sound as the dogs came upon the very spot I entered the water soon followed by men dressed in black.

I hid myself around the backside of the pole enduring the agonizing pain, which rendered me by the cramp. I waited; I waited wondering if they were going to come. The cramp had subsided and I began to look around for anything to further my escape, in that instant I found it. The timing could not have been any better for my captures had spotted me.

It was a boat. A small aluminum flat bottom boat well used but floating nonetheless and I urgently made my way to it pulling my body overboard nearly capsizing. After loosening the rope from the dock I was floating with the current. There was only one oar and I was thankful for every stroke it allowed me to be further from those in my pursuit. The men shouted indistinctly and the dogs howled viciously until I was well out of their vicinity.

I dug the parchment very carefully from my pocket and gently opened it. I spread it out across one of the seats giving it the possibility to dry. Inspecting it as it lay there I saw that Jonas knew more than I had thought. The map was of the surrounding area and gave direction to the safe city.

The city lay in my immediate direction and in that I found a minute amount of comfort. The map showed the river nearly being cut off by two great peaks and just after those peaks the city could be seen. How long had I been carried by the current? Will I ever see my brother again?

After bathing my wounded arm, rewrapping it, and drinking deeply of the water I tried to find a comfortable position. A therapeutic rhythm, produced by the river, lulled me in to a state of unconsciousness.

Chapter XIII

A dream came to me, as did the astute awareness of it being a dream. I knew it had specific meaning for I felt relief.

I saw something like a sea of glass mingled with fire, and many who deserved their victory standing on the glass all playing golden instruments and singing a song that drove through my soul with a shattering affect since one of those many was my brother.

The scent of death caused me to open my eyes. My parched lips starved for even the smallest droplet of water and I reached over the side of the boat, cupped a portion of liquid, filling my mouth, only to spit it out violently. Sitting erect in the boat I took stock of my surroundings. For a fleeting moment I was sure my eyes were playing some sort of foul prank on me but sight served correct. The river was blood red and every creature within was either floating or had lined the river's bank, all dead.

In the distance I could see the two peaks split the sky. Close I may have been but not close enough to become overwhelmed with excitement. I grabbed my lonesome oar and tried to paddle my way downstream with little to no gain. The floating dead lay too thick and my choices were slim. Fight the river or take to the land? I chose the latter.

Miles I had put beyond the boat when I started to regret my decision and my feet started to bleed. When I removed the shirt I had wrapped around my wounded arm, to cover my feet, I noticed the laceration had taken on a fever and was inflamed.

Night closed in catching me completely off guard. There were no stars, or moon, and I could see nothing. When a twig broke in the distance I knew I was not alone.

It is impossible to describe how nervous I felt. I did not want to move a muscle, yet I had to, I did not want to take a breath, yet I had to. Ever so quietly I crouched giving the ground light touches, making sound as minimal as possible, in search of a large stick or a rock, anything I could use as a weapon. I found nothing.

Lightning struck beyond the distant peaks taunting me, for that present time, with an unattainable goal of reaching them. How far were they, fifteen maybe twenty miles?

Thunder rumbled matching the sound of my beating heart and throbbing skull. My arm burned with fever and every moment standing my feet reminded me of their ailment. Unshaven, unclean, and my resent past had left me many pounds lighter making me quite feeble. I was in no condition to make fight but what choice does one have in a situation with no escape?

The footfalls of the one who approached me grew closer and I took a few steps backwards. My feet were bare and my bleeding toes clasped around what felt like a fallen branch. Quickly, yet, quietly I picked up a two-foot stick with my good hand. It did not feel strong enough for its intended purpose. Testing the strength with a bend I was careful but not careful enough for the stick snapped under the pressure and gave my location away with the sound.

Instantaneous to the sound of the snapping branch the footfalls came closer, rapidly closer as I awkwardly retreated backwards. My heel found an enormous obstruction coursing pain through my system and sending me falling to the ground. Even though I did find exactly what I had been looking for all that time in the dark, a large rock, I did not want to find it with the back of my head.

White spurts entered my field of vision, not from lightning, from the immense blow to the back of my head. I became dizzy and my mind began to wonder. My conscience was flooded by memories when I felt the spot where my head had made contact with the rock. It was the same spot, which seemed as if it were a lifetime ago, that I had slipped on the glass in my kitchen when frantically searching for my wife Fallon.

I felt deserted and alone. I did not wish for death but if my pursuer were too persuasive I would have accepted for I was in no condition to resist.

My leg was nudged my something large and soft. I heard a large exhale from an unmistakable creature, a horse.

Timidly I reached my hand in its direction and when touched the horse seemed to be as glad to feel me as I was to feel it. Fear subsided, moral restored, and in the pitch of night we stayed by each other's side enjoying the company of one another.

I was shivering fiercely by the time morning had come. My body ached and my wounds were growing worse. I was weak from the loss of blood and lack of food. If I were to survive I need to bathe my wounds and to find food immediately.

When inspecting the horse I found it was a mare. She had black leopard spots periodically placed on a roan background and white trim around her eyes. Her ribs were showing and I knew she was as hungry as I.

My feet were in bad shape and I tried to mount her but my strength was minimal and I could not pull myself to her height. Before I made another step she helped.

She must have been well trained for she couldn't help but notice my struggling effort, lowered down to her belly, and when I was astride she raised erect.

"Good girl." I said with great sincerity as we began to move in the peak's direction.

We kept the river well within view as we traveled. After several hours at a mild pace we came upon a large abandoned shack. The door was wide open and I was still in no condition to do much walking, so, with a little coaxing she walked me right through the door.

Immediately I was disappointed with what we had found. The place must have been deserted for several years. There seemed to be little but dust and decay residing within those dilapidating walls. With great effort I slid myself to the floor, hobbled my way around and pilfered through a few useless boxes. Upon opening one of the few remaining boxes I discovered a coiled snake, which struck me viciously on my wounded arm.

A sickness seeded itself into my inner being with the knowledge of my weakened condition not being able to withstand the snakebite. As I stepped back a three-foot snake made its way from the box making the mare more uneasy than myself. Angrily she snorted and stomped her foot on the floor. I knew if I didn't do something quickly she was going to hurt herself or me in due to the snake.

The snake was making its way in retreat when I grabbed it by the tail. It struck wildly at me missing its mark. I swung it like a whip ultimately smashing its head against the wall. Dead upon the floor I inspected it for fangs finding none. I did foresee it serving a great purpose, food.

Rummaging around through the cabinets I discovered two items that were going to enable me to start a fire, lighter with a good flint but no fluid and a few cotton swabs.

I had gathered debris from the boxes placing them in the stone fireplace talking calmly to the mare as I did so. After a while I thought she deserved a name other than girl so I began to call her Shiloh. Standing in the far corner she curiously watched my every move.

I unveiled a piece of metal sharp enough to help me prepare the snake for cooking. After all was in place I was ready to make a flame.

Taking a swab I gingerly fluffed parts of the cotton approximately a quarter inch away from the tip. Rolling the wheel that lay against the flint, ever so slightly without making a spark, particles of the flint collected on the cotton. When ample amount had gathered I moved it close to the debris and struck the wheel close to the flint-covered cotton, making spark. The sparks ignited the flint particles, which in turn ignited the fluffed cotton. Fire was made and after a short time so was dinner.

Before I took my first bite Shiloh had moved considerably close and knowing she would refuse I could not help but offer her some. With a snort, a snarled lip, and a step backwards I apologized for the gesture. With that being said I devoured nearly the entire snake saving some for later.

I could tell Shiloh was becoming restless and I promised her we would be well on our way as soon as I rested my eyes for a moment and then I heard the sound of howling dogs. The thought of being taken back to Strington crashed my mind causing me to shake uncontrollably. The knowledge of what they had done and what they would do to me made me move quickly.

Before I even realized I was mounted and we were hurdling through the doorway.

They were close, too close and when we came out the door Shiloh's chest knocked one man down and she trampled him with her back two hoofs crushing his bones as we sprang into the crisp evening air.

One of the dogs was let loose and it charged us making Shiloh buck nearly throwing me off her back. I held on desperately to her mane and heel her just below her haunches.

"Just take the mark and all of this will be over!" One of the men screamed.

"You're going to have to kill me!" I shouted meaning every word.

Two of the men had crossbows and let fly arrows. I felt pain in my shoulder; one had hit what he was aiming at. I broke the arrow leaving half inside me hoping it would slow the flow of blood.

In a flash we were gone, running for our lives towards the peaks. For a long while I had just let her run at full speed as the base of the peaks came into full view. I knew she was tired so I slowed her to a canter.

I began to thank her for helping me elude my captures I patted her and rubbed my hand down her side. There I found that the other man had hit his mark. Shiloh craned her neck and looked at me rolling her eyes as she did so. The arrow was embedded deep into her rib cage.

There was no way for us to make it over those peaks so we moved in the direction of the river. I hoped there was enough room between the base of the peaks and the river that we could make it through.

Fortunate we were to find hope materialize before our eyes as passage, as minimal as it was, opened creating a way through those peaks beside the river.

Shiloh's strength was failing fast for she began to limp and breathe heavily. If I were able to walk maybe she would have made it further than just beyond the passage.

The city was in view and I began to speak softly in her ear when she collapsed sending my body rolling upon the ground. I crawled to her side and shed many tears for the sacrifice she had made.

My friend had brought me many miles. Miles I am certain I would not have made on foot. Now she laid before me lifeless do to thirst and the wound given by the arrow. I could do nothing but thank her for what she had done for me and move on with my own death only a step behind.

The city's gates looked to be made of some kind of opaque quartz and loomed before me standing just over two hundred feet tall. The city illuminated the twilight as I momentarily stood in awe. I wanted nothing more than to be inside of those city walls. The thought of serenity, safety, and being amongst those I loved brought a feeling I had been without for a very long time.

An excitement gained control of actions making my body move faster than my feeble legs could keep up and I fell.

A force from beyond my knowledge brought me erect and I found myself standing in front of a horseman.

His face was illuminated to a brightness that made it impossible to decipher the contours of his face. He was dressed in some sort of white cloak. His horse was also white, not the white known to you and me, a white far surpassing any white imaginable. In his hand he held a golden book. For a moment he looked inside the book shuffling through a few pages, shook his head in a negative manner, and instantly the book ceased to exist.

I awaited the moment for a golden bow to materialize fulfilling a dream I had so long ago, instead his lips parted with a thunderous crash and like a two edged sword his words cut through my being, "Trials and tribulations you have surpassed, though, you have not the right to enter my city."

I felt the hand of death tighten its grip on me as the weight of my life pulled me to my knees. With every fiber within me I could not understand why, even after all that had happen, why I was not allowed through those gates.

"What do you mean I don't have the right?"

His voice gained a power beyond comprehension as he said his final words, "I KNOW YOU NOT!"

I was sure at that exact moment my final chance had arrived and my final breath was taken. A choice had to be made. With the air exhaling from my lungs I managed to utter two words, "Forgive me."

In that very instant the gates to the city opened and the inhalation of life filled me with the realization that my breath was given, not taken.

Surely I am coming quickly. Rev. 22:20

Printed in Great Britain
by Amazon.co.uk, Ltd.,
Marston Gate.